1

KATHERINE H. BROWN

Bake, Eat, & Be Buried

Ooey Gooey
Bakery Mystery
Book Three

Bake, Eat, and Be Buried

Written By: Katherine Brown

Cover Design By: Breezy Reads

Acknowledgments

As always, there are so many amazing people that I want to thank for being a part of this book's creation.

To my readers – you are some of the most wonderful people! You took a chance on my Ooey Gooey Mystery series & you came back for more. Thank you for all of the kind reviews & feedback.

To my family – aunts, uncles, grandparents, cousins, my parents, my husband, – thank you for your continued support and encouragement; thank you for buying my books, even when you have no time to read them, and for peddling them to your coworkers.

To Cammie M. & Ginger J. – my beta readers; thank you for taking the rough draft and reading through to help me polish up each page! You are indispensable.

To my fellow authors & CampNaNo cabin friends in Camper Canteen '19, thank you for the fun conversation, spirit of competition, and excellent encouragement that helped spur me to reach new goals.

~

Piper and Sam are flooded with ideas to help Flo's Flowers next door to have a spectacular 4th of July sale. However, plans get interrupted when the friends must prepare Piper to testify in court.

There is one major problem: Piper's fear of public speaking has her passing out!

Soon, a crowded room isn't the only thing Piper has to worry about.

Will she escape the tattooed man determined to shut her up permanently? Will the sheriff be able to help catch him after he hospitalizes one of her friends?

And, the biggest question of all, what is in the giant paper sack of "emergency supplies" that Gladys brings to the bakery?

~

Chapter 1

"I guess I should go get Kendra's flowers." Griff wiped his chocolate-coated fingers on a napkin. He moved to stand up from his stool at the large stainless-steel island in the kitchen.

"Flowers for Kendra?" Sam asked sharply, frowning at her brother.

"Wait, I'll go with you to Flo's to pick some out." Flo, a sweet lady in her early thirties, owned the flower shop next door to the bakery. "You should take some cookies, too." I tossed our trash into the can by the counter. "That's it!" I snapped my fingers together I just had a great idea that I want to run by Flo to help her summer business pick up."

"Cookies? For Kendra?" Sam waved her arms at us. "What are you two talking about?"

I laughed. "It's a long story. Watch the counter while I'm gone?"

"Sure," she grumbled. "I want to hear this idea for Flo's business when you get back though. And then when my big brother here stops loafing in our bakery and goes to work, you and I are going to talk." She put her hands on her hips and tried for a stern expression.

"Yes, ma'am." I saluted and she dissolved into smiles again. Walking to the door, I saw a now-familiar figure coming down the sidewalk. "I think this next customer is for you." I winked at Sam and headed next door with Griff. We smiled at Landon as he walked by, but continued forward on our mission.

"Piper! Griff! Hello," Flo smiled, but her eyes remained tired. "What brings you two by?" she asked.

"How are you, Flo?" Griff began. I had told him some of Flo's worries about her business.

"Getting by," Flo shrugged, her auburn bangs falling into her eyes. She pushed them back. "I shouldn't complain. Only this morning, in fact, I had some beautiful new daisies bloom."

"That's great," my enthusiasm may have been scaled up a bit much; Flo shot an odd half-smile my way. "Listen, we're actually here for two reasons," I told her. "Griff needs to buy some flowers and I wanted to talk to you about an idea of mine."

Flo lit up like a chandelier. "Flowers! Don't tell me this man finally asked you on a date and brought you to pick out your own flowers. Well, I've got some gorgeous roses right in this corner, follow me."

Really, has the whole town been waiting for Griff and I to date or what?

For such a petite woman, several inches shorter than me, Flo moved with the speed of a Nascar driver. Griff and I hurried to catch up.

"I don't think roses are what I need," Griff told her, as she held up a large vase filled with red and pink roses, sprigs of greenery, and some delicate white, twirly accent stems.

"They aren't for me," I added. "Griff needs something pretty, but not romantic."

Flo turned a quizzical frown our direction. "So, these flowers aren't for a date then?"

"They are," Griff trailed off into an awkward silence, rubbing a hand behind his neck. "But they aren't for Piper."

Flo's eyes bounced between us. I took pity on her and filled in the gaps. "So, you see," I said after explaining the situation the best I could, "Griff doesn't want to lead Kendra on just because he agreed to his mother's terms of going out to dinner with her. That's why he has to bring her flowers. Except," I tapped my finger on my chin, thinking, "except they need to be more like break-up flowers than first date flowers."

Flo nodded.

"And I'm going to stick some cookies into the bouquet."

Flo stopped nodding so fast that it looked like someone hit the pause button. "Cookies?" she cocked her head.

"That's right, cookies. Chocolate will ease the sting."

Her expression cleared as understanding dawned. "Good idea," Flo agreed. "Alright then, break-up flowers…let's see what I can do."

Griff and I milled about the front of the shop, admiring several pre-arranged bouquets, while Flo collected several cut flowers and carried them to her workroom in the back of the building.

"Which is your favorite?" Griff waved his hand at the room full of beautiful blooms.

"There are so many beautiful ones," I bent to sniff a bouquet of pink roses. "But I don't see my very favorite flower in here."

"No?"

I shook my head. "No. I love bell flowers. Bluebells, purple bells, orange bells – I can't place my finger on why, but they have always seemed stunning to me."

Flo rejoined us with a bright smile. "Never in all my years have I been asked for an order of break-up flowers. Here, what do you think of these?"

Griff looked to me; Flo's gaze followed as they awaited judgment.

Five bright yellow sunflowers were interspersed with smaller white mums and a few sprigs of green. The arrangement was not too large but still would fill a vase nicely. "Perfect," I smiled at Flo. The stems were tied with a loopy yellow ribbon. "There will be plenty of room to put maybe three cookies on long sticks and slide them into the ribbon as well."

Griff pulled out his wallet. "How much?" After settling the bill with Flo, Griff pulled me into a swift hug and left to go to work, leaving the flowers with me so that I could add some cookies to the arrangement for him. My stomach tightened at the thought of him going out with Kendra.

"You said you wanted to talk about an idea for my business?" Flo asked.

Grateful for the distraction, I bobbed my head. "If you have time," I watched her lock up and then followed her to the back room when she agreed.

"Okay." I thought about where I wanted to start as we sat down. "I actually had a couple of ideas, but you won't hurt my feelings if you don't like them."

"Girl, if it gets buyers in this door, I'll love them. What have you got?" Flo had a pen and paper out and a no-nonsense look. My desire to help her out doubled, buoyed by seeing that she hadn't decided to give up on her business by a long shot.

"Every place that I've seen does only flower bouquets or only cookie bouquets," I started. "I think we can team up to make a beautiful mixed bouquet of both live and cookie flowers. The cookies don't even have to be flower shaped, but they could, depending on what the customer needs the bouquet for."

Flo tilted her head. "How would we make the cookies part of the bouquet?"

We discussed options for a while, settling on the cookies being wrapped in cellophane and taped to long sticks. Flo had some ideas for stability to keep the cookies from being top-heavy and we agreed that I would deliver the cookie stems to her for all of the final arrangings. Cookies could be written on with icing to take the place of a card, or shaped into anything from flowers to sunshine, smileys, and more.

"This could be really fun," Flo's eyes sparkled. "You said you had more than one idea?"

~

I walked back to the bakery with, dare I say it, a spring in my step. Flo had been excited about the ideas and spoke in hopeful tones about her business again. It felt good to help others, a fact I had been reminded of when Sam and I did so much to fundraise money for Breaking Chains, one of many organizations fighting human trafficking, several weeks ago.

Samantha Lowe happened to be my best friend and co-owner of the Ooey Gooey Bakery where we worked. The business had taken off more quickly than we dreamed and just last weekend we had worked our first out-of-town catering event.

I pushed open the door and inhaled the sweet scent of ooey gooey deliciousness. The subtle fragrance of vanilla extract might be my favorite scent in the world. I waved to a few of our early morning customers and exchanged greetings on my way to the counter where Sam waited for me. I noticed the freshly painted tables were the buzz of most conversations.

"Millie's tabletop scenes are still a hit it sounds like," I tipped my head to all of the brilliant dancing cookies and gorgeous cupcakes painted in bright, beautiful colors.

"Are those the flowers for Kendra?"

"Yes. Aren't they nice? And *friendly*?"

"Spill it. Why is Griff giving Kendra flowers, why are you happy with it, and where do cookies come in?"

Saved from answering right away by a customer, I rang up an order for Grandpa Rex – the grandkids were getting Chocolate Oatmeal Cookies this week – and counted out change for him while Sam put the cookies in a to-go bag.

"You will recall that in exchange for information about what substance the canister held that got me hauled in for questioning, Griff had to make a deal with your mother?"

"Of course. The deal was that he takes Kendra to the Independence Day Parade though."

"True, but Griff is taking Kendra out tonight instead to explain things. I don't know what that will mean for the parade, Griff isn't the type to break his word, but he told me he wanted to get the date with Kendra over so that nothing stood in the way of him and me."

Sam shrugged. "Fine, he goes on a date with her. That doesn't explain the flowers and cookies and you...." Running out of words, Sam waved her hand up and down at me and then the flowers that were on the counter.

"Okay. Well, to be honest, I'm not happy with any of it, but I will not ask Griff to go back on his word. That would be wrong. The date includes the full works: flowers, dinner, wine, all of it. I helped with the flowers to make sure they didn't scream romance and you heard me suggest the cookies."

She crossed her arms and raised an eyebrow. "You suggested cookies because... you're now planning to resort to poison? Piper, you know there is no double jeopardy thing since you were never charged. If you poison my brother's date, you may go to jail. It might be hard to date Griff from jail. Also, I don't want to run the bakery without you."

I doubled over in laughter. Sam rang up two more customers while I tried to compose myself.

"I do not plan to poison Kendra. I do not plan to poison anyone," I stated as clearly as I could before sticking my tongue out at my friend. A bad habit for kids, worse that I'm an adult but what can I say, some habits aren't worth breaking. "I suggested the cookies because not only is this the first dinner date it will also be the last and only one; cookies will cushion the blow. After all, it isn't Kendra's fault that Deidra is a menace to the lives of both her children."

"Amen to that," Sam rolled her eyes.

I imagined thoughts of Deidra's reaction when Sam told her she planned to open the bakery with me were running through her head as they were mine. Deidra Lowe took her role as the mayor's wife of Seashell Bay very seriously. As in, seriously stuck up and concerned only with power and appearance. I shook my head, amazed at how Griff and Sam had turned out as normal, caring individuals when their mother groomed them to be political puppets for most of their childhood.

"I'm also glad you don't plan to poison people," Sam winked, successfully drawing me back to reality from my thoughts.

"That reminds me though, I need to tell you about the ideas Flo and I discussed that I think will eliminate her summer sales slump, and draw in some extra business for the Ooey Gooey as well."

"Great, Gladys called earlier and should be here shortly. She can watch the counter while we go talk about your plans and put some more cookies in."

"Perfect," I glanced at the door as the bell chimed above it. "Look, there's Gladys now."

Chapter 2

"Good morning girls!" Gladys hugged each of us in turn. "How did you enjoy your working weekend at The Cove's Cabins?"

I glanced at Sam. She looked back at me with big, round eyes.

"Tell me, you girls didn't get yourselves into trouble again did you? Piper? Sam?' the older woman narrowed her eyes as we stayed quiet.

She pursed her lips as seconds ticked by. My hands started to sweat; it felt like any minute now I would be grounded or something.

Sam tried to make a break for the register to help a customer, but Gladys steered them away, asking if they had seen the latest truffle flavors.

"Piper got us tied up and locked in a brothel," she blurted in a harsh whisper.

Gladys raised her eyebrows. I busied myself bagging up truffles and cookies for the teen at the register. I counted back the change to her slowly…in all pennies. Finally, I turned.

"Technically, it was a massage parlor," I pointed out.

For several minutes, we told Glady the condensed version of events from our harrowing weekend.

"I'm not sure it's safe for you two to leave the bakery," Gladys harrumphed at the end. "Then again, if trouble is going to find you, I'm happy for you to take it far from me."

We laughed. "How about you? Anything new or fun?" I asked.

"Nope."

Sam and I shared another look. We found out that Gladys had been going to cooking classes taught by none other than Chef Fabio, whom she and thirty other ladies had enjoyed ogling at the O Heavenly Day Spa several weeks prior. Gladys had a lifetime of cooking skills accumulated, so much so she could probably teach her own class. Truly, I think Chef Fabio's French accent more than his cooking had bewitched them all; regardless, Gladys was keeping this new class a secret for some reason that Sam and I hadn't yet figured out.

"Well, thanks for helping out at the bakery while we were away this weekend." Sam smiled.

"And for watching the counter today during lunch, too," I added. "Sam and I will be right in the back. Come get us if you need anything."

"Is there dough already chilled?" I asked as we stepped into the large kitchen.

"In the fridge. I'll preheat the oven and ready the pans."

I walked to the large walk-in fridge and snagged two bowls. Placing them on the counter, I scooped balls of Black and Whites onto the parchment-lined pan. Sam, in the meantime, made us each a glass of iced green tea. After the cookies were in the oven with the timer set, I sat down next to Sam at the large island work station.

"Do we need your notebook or have you already made lists?" Sam asked.

Sam knew good and well that I had already made several lists. I make lists of lists that need to be made. I find lists to be therapeutic. I ignored her, sniffing pointedly, as I pulled a slim notepad from the side pocket of my cargo pants.

"Do I at least get to see the list?" she smirked.

23

"No. You are obviously a doubter of the great good of lists and therefore unworthy of possessing said list."

"Fine," she tossed her hands up in defeat. "Please, read me your list. I really am curious how in the world we can help Flo sell flowers."

I explained to Sam my ideas about adding flower-shaped cookies to special occasion arrangements Flo makes. "Flo liked the idea, but where I think we can really boost sales are from Fourth of July Specials."

"What kind of specials? For us or for Flo?"

"Both." I put my notebook away and pulled out my phone. For this, visuals would help. "See all of the combinations of red, white, and blue flowers that can be made?" I scrolled down the screen.

"Those are extraordinary," Sam breathed.

I smiled. I knew this would be a good plan. "Exactly. And Flo has never used this holiday to increase store traffic before. It is a great opportunity though because tons of people are hosting parties and celebrations. Red, white and blue flowers would be a simple and elegant decoration. So, besides adding gorgeous Fourth of July bouquets, we are going to run a joint sale. Parties need cookies after all."

"Tell me about the sale."

"Anyone who purchases a Fourth of July bouquet from Flo's Flowers will receive a coupon for ten percent off of their Fourth of July cookie order!"

"That's brilliant!" Sam clapped. "I'll design some advertisements to place on the counter here and at Flo's so that the word gets out early."

"Thanks, Sam. That would be perfect."

The timer buzzed on the oven. Sam grabbed a pair of oven mitts and pulled the pans, sliding the cookie-laden parchment paper onto cooling racks. Delicious scents of chocolate filled the air as the room warmed slightly.

"Didn't Landon come in earlier?" I asked over my shoulder as I continued making a few more notes on my list. Landon was a friend from childhood who had recently popped back into my life. His sudden appearance, while confusing at first, was something else I was thankful for; I had been happy to see him again, doing well, and surprised to find out he had a career with Breaking Chains.

"Yes, he dropped in to see how we were doing. He said he had a few people to meet with in town and might stop by again later for some cookies."

"Cool," I stretched. "I think I'll go help Gladys with the register for a few minutes and check out the display case for empty spots."

~

We worked for most of the day baking, selling, and cleaning up. Business remained steady and gratefulness hummed inside of me.

At half-past four, Victoria rushed in. "Am I late?" she panted, heaving her book bag onto a chair.

"Not at all. You're just in time to help me bake up some practice cupcakes." I smiled at the teen. She and her friend Millie had been lifesavers, helping Gladys with the bakery while Sam and I had been catering at the retreat over the weekend. I had been excited to see Victoria's text this morning asking if we still needed part-time help. She had great ideas in the kitchen and I hoped to help boost her confidence.

We walked through the swinging door from the café part of the bakery into the kitchen. I stopped short, surprised to find Millie and Sam huddled over a laptop.

"Hey, Millie! Did you come to help bake, too?"

"No way!" She shook her head quickly. "That is definitely all Victoria. You know my skills in the kitchen are limited to opening the refrigerator door, and even that goes wrong sometimes." We all chuckled.

"I invited Millie here to help with the advertisements and flyers for our holiday promotion," Sam explained, a twinkle in her eye. "I'm going to handle the actual wording and layout but after seeing her artwork first-hand...."

"Sam's letting me do the graphics!" Millie bounced up and down, long blonde ponytail swaying back and forth.

My heart warmed that Sam had obviously developed a soft spot for the two girls, also, and my smile grew. "That sounds awesome," I told them. "Millie, you should know, the beautiful tables that you painted are still receiving compliments."

"Thanks," she beamed.

"Do you have any other art assignments coming up? Ones where you will need to paint something large?"

Millie tilted her head and thought a moment. "I just might," she said. "I'll double-check the syllabus but I think we had to do three projects this summer."

"Let me know. I have another idea for you." Victoria and I moved to the pantry and pulled out the ingredients we would need.

"What kind of practice cupcakes are we making?" Victoria asked, eyeing the ingredients with suspicion.

"Red Velvet Blueberry Cheesecake Cupcakes!"

Just then, Gladys poked her head through the door. "Piper...." She stepped aside as a deputy pushed his way into the room.

"Piper Rivers?" he asked.

I wiped flour from my hands and stepped forward. "Yes. May I help you?"

The man thrust a folded paper into my hands. "You've been served."

Chapter 3

Gladys peeked back into the café. "Everyone is cozy. Go ahead and open it." She waited along with Sam, Victoria, and Millie, each of them watching as I tore open the envelope.

I scanned the page, my eyes roving up and down until finally, I released the breath I had been holding. "It's a subpoena to testify," I answered the unspoken question on everyone's face.

"Testify about what?" Victoria asked.

"That, that is a long story."

~

Hours later, I yawned. "I'm beat." I wouldn't tell Sam, but mentally I was a wreck, too. The words of the subpoena were burned into my brain: **You are hereby summoned to be and**

personally appear at 8:00 AM on the 27th day of June 2019 before the Pierson County District Court to testify and to speak the truth....

"It has seemed like a long first day back at the Ooey Gooey," Sam nodded in agreement. "Ready to call it a night?"

I stirred and blinked to clear my head. "Yep. I think it's time I headed home to my own cozy bed."

Sam shot me a side-glance. "Have you heard from Griff?"

"Not yet." I turned out the lights.

"Have you texted him to see if his date with Kendra is over?"

"Not yet." I locked the back door as we left the bakery.

Sam laughed. "Would you be interested in stalking the town to see if we can find them?"

"I thought you would never ask!"

"Come on," she linked her arm through mine and steered me to her yellow Juke.

Driving through our quaint little town, we scanned the parking lots of the top three best restaurants, Oyster House, Roadhouse, and Momma's Diner, but didn't see Griff's truck at any of them. We passed the movie theater with a much more crowded parking lot than I expected for a Monday night.

"I don't think they would have gone to a movie," I said.

"Me neither. Let me think, surely not fast-food chains either." Sam pulled into a gas station to fill up.

"I've got it!" Getting back in the car, Sam drove us down to the marina. A few small boats were moored at their docks, along with two larger yachts. Fishing trawlers were still out for the evening it looked like.

"The boat docks?"

"No." Sam pointed to a well-lit building teeming with fancy cars in the parking lot. "The Daily Catch."

I looked. Sure enough, Griff's truck sat high above the swanky sports cars in the lot. Being so far from the hubbub of town, not to mention outrageously priced, I always forgot this restaurant existed way out here.

"How did you know Griff would be here? Is the food that good?"

"The food is that good, but that isn't why Griff brought Kendra here."

I waited. "Well? Why here then?"

Sam turned the car back around to the highway, angling back toward the heart of the town. "Maximum exposure," Sam said as she merged onto the road. "Mother would have received a text, maybe even a phone call, the moment Griff walked in those doors. This is where her Catamaran Club meets. Only the social aristocracy have memberships to The Dailey Catch."

The ride back to pick up my truck stayed quiet. Lost in thought, our arrival came quickly and took me by surprise. Sam's reasoning for Griff made sense; still, I had lost my appetite and planned to crawl into a book and hide for a few hours when I got home.

"See you tomorrow," Sam called through her open window as I climbed into my beautiful blue truck. I waved and, with a prayer, turned the key. The truck rumbled to life and I said a sincere thanks as I drove home. *One day, I'm going to have to get the starter checked for a short.*

Getting lost in a book turned out to be harder than planned. Every few minutes, rather than the words on the page, I kept picturing the subpoena again. I couldn't believe that I had been called to testify. Me. Only me. I mean, my goodness, there were multiple of us tied up in that room. Why did the prosecution think that I could make some big difference at Regina's trial?

Giving up on finding out whether or not Prince Charming overcame his beastly curse and met his princess, at last, I put away my book and punched the pillows into submission. Falling into a fitful sleep, I dreamed that the judge sentenced me to prison for not being able to explain how to bake a perfectly risen souffle for his wife's birthday.

~

The next morning, I awoke more nervous about testifying than ever; now I feared being put back in jail for no reason. The temperature hit seventy-five degrees out before I got to the Ooey Gooey Goodness Bakery at five to start baking. I tossed my hair up in a short ponytail and turned on the fan in the kitchen. Sam stepped inside shortly after me.

"Wow! Your hair looks amazing in that braid." I stepped closer to admire it. "The red kind of twirls all through it like woven ribbon."

"Thanks," Sam smiled as she tied her apron strings around her neck. "I couldn't stand to have it down today. Looks like our summer heat wave is really cranking up."

"Definitely."

"Speaking of hair…are you going to keep your gorgeous turquoise and silver? If so, I need to schedule you an appointment with Lainey to touch them up soon. They are fading a bit and it isn't as pretty without the turquoise."

Sam never pulled punches, but I knew that in her own way she said it to be helpful. "You know, that would be great thanks. I've grown pretty attached to the colors."

"Told you," Sam winked. I had only dyed the tips of my hair as a prank to get her to stop bothering me about *boring* hair. The joke was on me because it turned out awesome and I really loved it.

"What about you? Surely by now Deidra has grown used to your red layer of hair? She might even consider it *normal*." I mock-gasped; Sam's only rebellious streak against her uppity mother's fashion-obsessed upbringing happened when she started dyeing her hair in college. It gave Deidra fits for her daughter to have "unnatural" har which we found hilarious considering Deidra had been covering up her gray roots for longer than I'd known her.

"I have something big in mind. When Victoria and Millie are here again later this week, I'll tell you."

We finished the baking in record time, and Sam went out front to unlock the door. After setting the last cookies out to cool, I carried out two glasses of tea and joined her.

"When do you have to appear in court?" she asked as we sat down at one of the tables.

"Thursday, day after tomorrow. I'm kind of nervous."

"It'll be like answering a few questions in a conversation; a fairly one-sided conversation. And then it'll be over before you know it. I know you hate to speak in front of crowds, but how many people could it be anyway?"

Chapter 4

A lot. A whole lot of people, that's how many. Wednesday had passed in a blur of busy baking and Thursday was upon us already. Thankfully, Sam and Griff were numbered among the crowd. They would be here for me when this was all over.

I was seated in the second row of benches with several people I didn't know, and one or two familiar faces including my friend Landon and Roy, the caretaker from The Cove's Cabins. I took a deep breath and tried to calm my mind.

"All rise for the Honorable Judge Rickson," the bailiff bellowed.

I stood along with everyone else. My palms poured sweat as did my underarms; boy, I hoped I put enough deodorant on today. Soon, the judge asked everyone to be seated other than those of us who would be testifying.

"Raise your right hand," he ordered.

We did. I thought it strange that they would swear us in as a group, but that is exactly what happened. Before I knew it, our oath finished and we were led out into the hallway. I didn't realize that if you were giving testimony, you weren't allowed to sit in the courtroom for any other part of the trial.

"There is to be absolutely no talking," the woman who seated us outside instructed. "Remain at least one foot apart at all times." With that, she re-entered the courtroom. I could see her stationed on alert inside the doors.

One at a time, my companions on the hall bench were called and led inside, then escorted back out to sit and wait. *Maybe they will decide they don't need my testimony. Maybe the trial will be over before they anticipated.* I watched enough TV to know that I was kidding myself. These things could last for days or weeks. *Oh God, please don't let this go on for weeks.* As I dreaded, my turn eventually came.

"Piper Rivers," the doorwoman called in the same bored, monotone voice she had used each time she retrieved a witness.

"Hi!" I tossed my hand up in a small wave, instantly regretting letting my nervousness take over as the doorwoman glared at me as if I'd just shot her a rude gesture. *Great, I'm not supposed to be talking,* I remember; now I'll probably get arrested for disobeying the judge or something crazy. I dropped the smile and averted my gaze from the doorwoman, walking past her, back into the courtroom, and down the side aisle to the box where the bailiff held the short swinging door open for me.

"Miss Rivers, I would like to remind you that you are under oath. Please affirm that you understand and that you swear to tell the truth," the bailiff asked as I entered the box.

"I do...understand that is, I understand and um, I will..." my eyes slipped to the room before me. Faces swam before me, a blur of eyes on me. "Is it hot in here?" I struggled to draw breath.

~

I blinked. Opening my eyes wide, I spotted dirt gray ceiling tiles. *Ceiling tiles?* The sea of faces was gone. I blinked again and heard voices approaching.

"Piper, are you okay?" Sam's face loomed over mine.

Griff appeared on my other side and helped me to sit up.

"I'm good. What…are we still at the courthouse?"

"Yes. You fainted when you sat down to testify. Thankfully, the bailiff was still standing close and prevented you from hitting your head or anything."

Griff picked up where Sam stopped, "They brought you into one of the antechambers. A paramedic should be here any minute."

"I don't need a paramedic," I grumbled. "I'm just an idiot scared of public speaking."

"You are not an idiot. I don't want you to talk like that," Griff rubbed my back and massaged my shoulders. I could get used to this. No wonder you were always reading books about women in the middle ages passing out at the drop of a hat; if they were coddled later, who could blame them.

"Hey!" I jerked upright from my relaxed posture. "You never told me about the date with Kendra."

Griff had been booked with multiple inspections yesterday so he hadn't stopped at the bakery. Sam and I spent big portions of the day fine-tuning our plans to team up with Flo for some summer sales and I hadn't had time to pester Griff with texts or phone calls.

A door opened and a fresh-faced boy with a light blue paramedic uniform hustled to my side. He placed his fingers on my wrist, checking my pulse.

"Don't worry, I'm alive," I quipped. He only nodded and continued with his check-up. After I answered an onslaught of questions concerning how I felt, what I'd eaten, if me passing out ever happened before and so on, the young man cleared me to go home for the day and left.

Before I could go anywhere, the bailiff came in. "Miss Rivers, I've been instructed to inform you that trial has gone into recess and will resume next Monday morning at eight. You are to be here and be ready to testify or be held in contempt." A swift turn on his heel and he retreated from the room.

Cradling my head in my hands, I sighed. What in the world was I going to do? The thought of getting back up in front of the room full of people made my head spin and my stomach nauseated.

"Let me take you home," Griff spoke as we exited the courthouse.

Sunshine spilled across the steps and I inhaled a deep breath of the warm, salty air. "No," I said with a shake of my head. "I feel completely fine now and there is too much to do at the bakery. Please, drive me back there."

He agreed and we began the trek across the road and parking lot to his truck, Sam by my side. As we rounded the end of a gray van, a man walked straight into me from behind, separating me from Sam and causing me to stumble into Griff.

"Hey!" Griff yelled at the man while trying to steady me with both hands. The man took off at a run and jumped into a waiting white Mercedes. They sped away.

"Sam," he looked to his sister as she glared after the fleeing car. "Sam, are you okay?"

"I'm fine. Piper, check your purse. We may have been mugged." She flipped open her purse and searched its contents. "My wallet is still here. Phone, keys, pepper spray, lipstick, everything I think."

My wallet and phone, normally kept in my cargo pant pockets, hadn't fit in those of my slacks so I'd been forced to use a purse to carry them to court today. I opened the mouth of the purse wide and dug around. "Phone, wallet, keys, phone, gum…wait a minute." I reached back into the purse and handed out the contents to Sam and Griff one at a time. Sure enough, there were two phones.

My own phone, a touchscreen smartphone with the saying 'Life is short, lick the spoon,' on the case went back in my purse with the wallet and other items, but I held onto the strange little red flip-phone. When it rang seconds later, I nearly had a heart attack.

"Hello?" I answered.

"Pity, passing out on the stand. Testifying might be dangerous for your health, don't you think?"

"Excuse me?" I received no response; the caller had disconnected.

"Let's get in the truck," I told Griff and Sam, walking that direction before they had time to object.

"Who was that on the phone?" Sam asked.

"That man dropped it in your purse on purpose, didn't he?" Griff's voice hardened. Something in my face must have given it away. I refused to look back. I had to get to the truck, get my friends in the truck, and process this somewhere out of the open.

We hopped in the truck, me in the passenger seat and Sam in the back. Griff cranked it and drove out of the parking lot, stopping at the exit to pass the parking stub to the attendant and pay.

"Yes," I said fingering the phone in my hand. "I'm certain this phone was the reason that man jostled me in the parking lot. I don't know who it was, but they must have been in court today." I relayed the cryptic conversation.

"I'll drive you to the police station."

"What? Why?" I asked Griff.

"Piper, you can't be serious. You need to turn that phone in. Maybe the police can pull a print or something."

"I agree with Griff," Sam said. "Which obviously means you are going to disagree if we're judging by our recent track record."

"No, I know. You're both right." I touched Griff's arm as he started to flip the blinker on. "Please, can we go to the bakery first and grab a snack? Give me a short time to think about who it could be, then maybe when we take it to the police, I'll have some other thoughts or information to share with them, too. I'm sure I've smudged any prints by now anyway, so what could a few more hours hurt?" I gave him my best puppy-dog eyes, even though I hadn't perfected them over time as Sam had.

"I got a partial plate on the car I think," Sam spoke up from the backseat a while later. "At least, I tried. It was hard to read since they were going so fast, but I believe it started with CA1."

"I'm impressed, Sis." Griff eyed her in the rearview mirror.

"Thanks. That was when I still thought the guy might've nicked something from our purses."

"What doesn't make sense to me is, I thought Regina was calling the shots on trafficking those women at the Thai Massage Parlor. If she's in custody, who would be out here worrying about me? Another goon? Or a bigger fish?" I crossed my arms and leaned back in my seat, mulling it over.

"Goon? Fish? Have you been watching mobster shows?" Griff laughed.

Nobody seemed in the mood for any conversation. Eventually, we pulled into the lot behind the Ooey Gooey Goodness Bakery.

Sam scooted out of the seat and made her way to the back door.

I lingered.

Griff combed rough fingers through my hair, sweeping it behind one ear. "I have to go to work," he said. "Promise me you will take that phone to the police."

"I will."

"Today."

"Later today." *Much, much later* I thought to myself. "Yes, I will."

"Hey," I remembered what was niggling at the back of my brain as I opened the door. Turning back, I asked, "How did dinner with Kendra go?"

"It went fine. She loved the flowers, especially when I told her my girlfriend picked them out. She's looking forward to meeting you."

I shook my head and waved as he drove off with a grin. Boy, to have been a fly on the wall for that conversation. I'd pull it out of him though, sooner or later.

My steps were considerably lighter as I made my way into the bakery. "Blessed air conditioning," I smiled as a wave of cool air hit me. Things were heating up fast outside.

"Oh good! You're here. Taste this," Victoria appeared in front of me with a spoon.

Taking it, I shoved a full bite of cream into my mouth and let it sit. "Butterscotch and coconut?" I asked, running my tongue over the roof of my mouth to explore the lingering hints of flavor.

"Yes. What do you think?"

"It's surprising but yummy," I told her honestly. "What is it going to be for though?" I couldn't for the life of me imagine what Victoria had come up with today. The girl was a fountain of experiments and ideas; most of them turned out to be delectable. Between her natural baking talent and her willingness to cover the bakery so that she could gain experience, Victoria was turning out to be a Godsend.

"I'm going to do a twist on an Oatmeal Cream Pie and make Butterscotch Oatmeal Coconut Cream Pies instead."

I stared at her a moment, the picture coming together in my head.

"You don't think it's a good idea?" she took the spoon back from me and tossed it in the sink dejectedly.

"Victoria, I think it is brilliant! I imagined them, the textures and flavors, and already my mouth is watering." I placed a hand on her shoulder. "Please let me know the moment they are done; I want to taste the first one."

The teen rewarded me with a mile-wide smile. "You got it!" She turned to the cabinets, already collecting mixing bowls and measuring cups.

Knowing she wouldn't need me for a bit, I pushed through the swinging door into the café to find Sam and Millie conspiring again, bent over a table with papers spread before them.

"Where's Gladys?" I asked, not seeing her behind the counter or among the tables of customers.

"She excused herself for a while when I got here. I believe she mentioned a few errands that would take her hours to complete." Sam raised her eyes up and down suggestively and slid me her phone.

"Ah, gotcha." I handed the phone back after seeing that Sam had looked up the schedule for cooking classes with Chef Fabio at the Senior Citizen Center. According to the schedule posted online, the next class would start in fifteen minutes. It would last for two hours. "Did Victoria tell you about her next cookies?"

"Yes. They sounded great."

"She's been baking since we were like twelve," Mille smiled. "I can't tell you what it means to her that you've given her a job here. Well, both of us really. And to think, we thought we just wanted a quick job and money for electric scooters."

"Did you get them?" Sam asked.

"Yes, we earned enough over the weekend, combined with the slight advance you gave us, to buy them. But really, we've gotten so much more than that working with you guys. Not many people would let two teenagers come in and trust them with the projects you've given us."

"It has been our pleasure to have you here," I assured her. "You've both worked your tails off and are doing an amazing job. Speaking of, what are we working on here today?"

"Millie brought the graphics for us to choose one to use in the flyers advertising the flower/cookie sale."

"Did you pick one?"

"No, I thought that you and Flo should have a vote before we decided. Why don't you tell me which is your favorite and then I'll go next door and ask Flo? I've picked mine." Sam held three papers up for me to look at.

"This one," I waved the middle page and handed them back. "Though they all look incredible, Millie."

"Thanks," she blushed.

"Sam," I added as they began to clear the table. "You mentioned you had a new idea for your hair?"

"That's right!" The grin that spread across her face held so much mischief, I found myself worried.

"Tell me you aren't chopping it all off?" I begged. Even to poke at Deidra, that would be going too far.

"Nope. I'm going to issue a challenge on the flyers. If Flo sells 150 arrangements and those people bring their coupon by and all purchase Fourth of July cookies, then I will dye my hair patriotic before the Independence Day Parade."

She and Millie breezed out the door before I could formulate a response. The only one currently running through my head was: *Patriotic hair? What does that even mean?* Followed immediately by *150 arrangements! There are only ten days until the Fourth of July.*

I worked the register for the rest of the afternoon. We were still getting a lot of moms in, bringing in kids for a summer treat. Sam and Millie popped back in just long enough to tell me they had finalized the flyer design and were going to make copies and start hanging flyers.

"Bring some back here first," I told them. "That way I can start telling customers right away."

"Will do, be back soon," Sam agreed.

As the crowd dwindled, I stuck my head through the door to the kitchen to check on Victoria. "How're things going?" I called. "Sorry!" I cringed as the girl jumped.

"It's okay. I was really concentrating and didn't hear you come in. I'm almost finished," she gestured at the stations of cookies, cream, and finished creations spread out before her in an assembly-line manner. "Things took a little longer because on the first cookie it the butterscotch coconut cream all leaked right out the sides; it needed to be thickened up just a smidge." She wiped her hands on the towel in her apron. "I think I've got it now though."

"Good for you," I glanced back into the bakery as the bell over the door tinkled. "Why don't you bring a small sample plate up front when you finish? Then you and I can try them and get the opinions of a few customers, too."

Back in the café, I greeted the man who had entered. He was new, or at least not someone I recognized and I think I would have remembered the eyebrow piercing. "Good afternoon, how can I help you?" I asked him.

Rather than acknowledge me, he looked around the room. Apparently satisfied that we were alone, he stalked forward. "Are you the owner?" His voice, gruff and low, was difficult for me to understand.

"I'm one of the owners," I said slowly as I gave him another look. A tattoo peeking from under his short sleeve caught my eye. Odd. I looked at the man's face again, confirming he didn't look at all familiar. Yet, that tattoo…. *Oh my gosh,* I thought when it clicked. The yellowed-teeth and angular chin visible at the bottom of the tattoo, an evil grimace, resembled the demon mask tattoo the man at the massage parlor had sported. What was his name? Ansil? Asana? No that was a yoga pose. Asnee! That was it.

"I said, are you Piper," the man ground out. Evidently, I hadn't been paying attention. He looked ticked.

"Yes, I'm Piper. Who are you?" It definitely wasn't Asnee standing in front of me, but that gave me no feeling of relief. If I were to guess, this guy didn't come in to buy a cupcake.

Eyebrow-ring guy took two menacing steps forward and I was happy to have the counter between us. Still, there was nowhere to go and I wouldn't let him in the back room with Victoria. Why the heck did we never put one of those silent-alarm -button thingies in under the register that called the police or someone to handle problem customers?

"Listen," I stood very still. "I'm not sure what it is you need, but if you don't plan to make a purchase, I'm going to have to ask you to leave. Now, if you're hungry, I personally recommend the Turtle Brownies. They will fill you up in no time."

The man growled and lunged, pulling a butterfly knife from his back pocket. I jumped back and the man grunted as he barreled into the counter. I fumbled for my own knife, clipped to a pocket in my pants and moved steadily away from the door to the kitchen.

The man sneered when I finally got my knife open with sweaty, fumbling fingers. As he stalked around the edge of the counter, I dodged and darted away. Just then, the bell on the door tinkled. My heart sank as I heard Sam's voice and dared a glance over to see her fiddling in her purse head down.

"Piper, I've got these flyers for you," she walked halfway into the room before she looked up.

"Sam, run!" I tried to warn her. Angry guy had turned when the door opened and looked torn between roughing me up or stopping her from leaving. Deciding I was the more pressing matter, the girl holding the small knife, he kept coming toward me.

I pushed a chair between us which he swept aside. I prayed Sam would go get help but the door remained silent. Scared to take my eyes off the immediate threat, I didn't see her getting closer.

"Hey ugly!" Sam yelled. As the man turned to her with a scowl, she doused him with pepper spray. I mean, she must have shot the whole can at him.

He dropped the knife. I scooped it up as it clattered toward me.

Sputtering and snarling the man lunged at Sam. I threw my knife at him.

It probably would have worked better if I actually had real knife throwing skills, though I'm considering acquiring some; still, the knife grazed his shoulder and being assaulted from two sides convinced him to change course; he veered out the exit.

Sam locked the door and leaned against it, her head tilting back as she took deep breaths.

I bent to pick up my knife, folding it closed. Victoria came into the café at that moment with a plate full of cookies and a giant smile. "Are you ready to taste these babies?" The grin slipped from her face as she looked at the disheveled room. Tables and chairs were out of place, several desserts in the display case were knocked askew.

Plus, there was the glare Sam rained down on me, making things awkward.

"I know, I know. The police," I held up my hands, each still grasping a knife, in surrender. "You know what Victoria?" I turned away from Sam and walked over to the speechless girl and snagged a cookie from the plate. "I'm definitely ready to try one of these. Maybe two."

I bit into the ooey gooey goodness, pastry cream ringing my mouth, and ignored the looks being shot my direction.

Chapter 5

"Yes, sir," I nodded for the hundredth time to Sheriff Kent. The moment I had finished my cookie, and Sam finished hers, she had ushered me to the car and driven me to the sheriff's department to report the latest happenings.

Since Sheriff Kent had played a big part in helping rescue me from a psychopathic bride-wanna-be kidnapper not long ago, I felt comfortable talking to him.

"All that happens by putting yourself in the place of law enforcement is trouble," he said again.

I nodded. Again.

"You say you are the only person who has handled this phone since it was dropped into your purse?"

"That's correct. Though I'm afraid as much as I touched it, I probably obliterated any evidence that was on it."

"And how long after the incident in the courthouse parking lot, clear in another county may I add, did this man try to attack you in your bakery?" The sheriff leaned back in his black leather chair and tapped his fingers on the arm of his chair.

I took a moment to think about the day. "Several hours," I shrugged.

"And do you believe it was the same man?"

"Honestly, I have no idea. I hadn't thought of that. I mean why go to all the trouble of dropping me a burner phone if he planned to expose himself out in the open?"

"I couldn't tell if it was the same person either," Sam added. "The guy in the parking lot had on long sleeves and a cap."

"And Miss Lowe, when you came back to the bakery this afternoon, did you happen to see the white Mercedes anywhere nearby that you saw picking up the man in the ball cap this morning?"

"I didn't notice it, but I wasn't exactly looking either."

Leaning forward in his chair, the sheriff gave us each a long look. When he spoke, he said,

"I think that's it, for now, ladies, but if anything else happens, I need to know. In the meantime, I'm going to have our tech guy take a look at this phone. Maybe, just maybe, there's still something we can find out from it."

"Yes, sir," I agreed.

"Thank you for your time Sheriff Kent," Sam stood and shook his hand.

Sam and I exited the sheriff's department and went straight to her car. For a moment, we simply sat.

"What now?" Sam asked.

"Are you hungry? I missed lunch today and I could go for some chicken or a burger."

"Sounds like a plan." Sam cranked the car and maneuvered out of the tiny lot. "Momma's Diner here we come," she said.

Chapter 6

We returned to the bakery after a delicious late lunch of burgers, fries, and milkshakes. Momma's Diner makes the best milkshakes in the South and I've had more than my fair share. The Triple Chocolate Quake Shake today did not disappoint.

"Now, I'm ready to collapse in a nice food coma." Sam rubbed her stomach as we walked into the bakery from the front. Sam chose to park on the street so she could work out of the box of flyers in her car, posting them up and down the storefronts surrounding us.

I bobbed my head in agreement. "Maybe splitting that second order of fries was going overboard."

"Hello girls," Gladys greeted as we drew near to the counter.

"Gladys! Thanks for coming back to cover the register when we had to rush off." Sam smiled.

"Think nothing of it. Victoria brought me up to speed on everything and I feel terrible that I wasn't here when that horrid man accosted Piper."

"Has Millie not returned?" I didn't see the budding artist; she had continued on the mission to post flyers around town while Sam and I took care of business at the sheriff's department.

Gladys shook her head. "Not yet. She texted Victoria to say she was almost done not long ago. That reminds me, Flo called and said she needs to talk to you, Piper. She was upset and it sounded urgent."

Worried that Flo might be having second thoughts about our ideas to help the flower shop flourish, I hurried next door.

"Flo?" I called out.

"In the back."

Flo pulled me further into the room when I entered, all the way to the back door which was propped open a crack with a spool of ribbon.

"Flo, Gladys told me you called."

"Shh…come here."

I joined her at the door, tiptoeing over as seemed appropriate given Flo's furtive peeking out the back door.

"What are we looking at?" I asked.

"I think he's gone now, but you never know if he might come back."

"Who?" My eyebrows formed a vee as I tried to puzzle out what Flo was talking about. So far, I was lost as a goose. *Do geese get lost often?* I frowned further; I'd never understood who invented all the odd sayings we used, but they sure stuck in your head.

"Are you listening?" Flo interrupted my meandering thoughts. "There was a man out back. He's gone now, but he was all over your truck."

"My truck?" I poked my head out the back door again. Still, nobody to be seen. I knew I kept it locked so I wasn't worried the man had stolen anything.

"Yes. I was taking a small bag of trash out – those flower stems start to stink pretty quickly if you don't dispose of them – and saw him poking around. He was crawling out from under it and I ran back inside as fast as I could. I don't think he saw me."

This didn't bode well. I knew one thing; the sheriff would want to hear about it.

~

Griff pulled up beside the curb about a minute after the sheriff had arrived and roped off the employee parking lot behind the bakery. Deputies swarmed my truck, going over it with various instruments.

I wrapped my arms around Griff and he rested his chin on my head. "See," I tilted my head toward the scene. "I called the sheriff."

"Please, tell your girlfriend not to engage in a knife fight with unsavory criminals." Sam joined us, hands on her hips.

"I see," I retorted before Griff responded. "You would prefer they were savory criminals? And would that be in reference to their smell or what exactly? I'll admit, there was a bit too much menthol cigarette smoke wafting from him for my tastes."

"How about no knife fights at all?" Griff squeezed me a little tighter, effectively ending what could have turned into hours of sarcastic banter.

"You take all the fun out of everything," I told him.

A small, lopsided grin broke free of the worried expression on his face.

"I sent Gladys and the girls home. Locked up the bakery, too." Sam watched as one deputy called the sheriff over to look at something. They knelt on the ground a minute before the sheriff held out a clear baggy and the deputy dropped something inside.

"Thanks. Looks like that was probably for the best," I freed myself from Griff's grasp and linked arms with the two of them. "Come on. Let's go see what they've found."

Flo, after giving her statement and a description of the man, had decided to remain inside her shop. I didn't blame her. My stomach somersaulted; my nerves were as frayed as the ends of a rough-cut rope, yet curiosity stirred up inside of me as well.

"Sheriff," Griff stuck his hand out and shook hands with Sheriff Kent as we met him in the middle of the parking lot. Deputies were beginning to load things back into the trunk of a police car.

Well, that's good, right? They finished quickly and nobody looks terribly worried.

"Miss Rivers, I'm afraid I have some bad news."

So much for good. Thanks for sugarcoating it, sheriff. I braced myself for the sheriff's next words.

Chapter 7

"A bug?" I jutted my head forward, determined to make sure I had heard the sheriff correctly.

"Yes, ma'am. Similar in model to the bug my tech guy pulled off the red burner phone planted in your purse. This type is used as a tracking device."

"Are you serious? Do people really do that? I thought that was all an exaggeration on tv shows where you see criminals accessing the latest tech and using it to beat the good guys."

"It wasn't exactly high-grade stuff," the sheriff conceded. "But it probably gave them your location at the bakery today. Since that didn't work, your perp came back to bug your truck. It seems likely they planned to try another run at you at your home." Sheriff Kent rubbed one hand along his scruffy jawline.

"I don't like this," Griff took my hand and squeezed. "That could easily have been a bomb planted instead of a bug. Sheriff, can you post a patrol at the bakery and at Piper's home? We need to make sure nobody is getting near her."

"Or she can come to stay with me," Sam suggested.

"No. I'm not putting anyone else in danger, I'll stay at my own place. Thank you," I told her. "I appreciate it. But the sheriff has the bug, this creep won't know where to find me now anyway."

"Write down the address," Sheriff Kent said over my head to Griff. "I'll dispatch a unit to make regular rounds at Miss River's home this evening."

"Thank you," Griff walked to his truck for paper.

The sheriff and his deputies finished up in no time. In possession of my address, the sheriff warned me to be aware of my surroundings and to call if there was trouble before they left.

"Ready to call it an early night?" Sam looked at me and Griff.

I checked the time on my phone and saw that I had a new text. "Nope. Gladys invited us over for supper. Says she has already cooked it and that there is no point in saying no."

"Do you think she'd mind one more?" Griff asked.

"You're her favorite," I smirked. "I doubt she will mind a bit."

~

Sam pulled her car into the driveway. I parked my truck at the curb of the canary-yellow bungalow and waited for Griff who had to park further down the block.

"House kind of matches her personality, doesn't it?" He asked as he strolled up with his hands in his jean pockets.

"Yep. And Sam's Juke, too," I joked.

"Very funny," she shouted from up the walkway.

Griff and I stepped onto the front porch the same time as Gladys opened the door. Following Sam inside, I inhaled deeply. "Something smells incredible," I said, hugging Gladys.

"It's just a little something," she tisked, waving a hand. Leading us into the kitchen, she asked about the truck and the sheriff and we each filled her in on the findings.

"And you're really going to stay at your apartment alone anyway?" Gladys wanted to know.

"I'll be fine," I insisted.

"Stubborn," Griff muttered under his breath.

Once seated at the table, Gladys took the covers off of several dishes. "Grilled Niçoise Tuna Steak, Vegetable Tian, and a Roasted Nut Green Bean Salad."

"I'm sorry, knee-shwah what?" I asked in an attempt to copy the strange new word describing our Tuna. "You're going to have to interpret that for me." I looked at Gladys expectantly.

"Niçoise, it's only a fancy word for French, dear. Now dig in."

Sam raised the ever-arcing eyebrow and shot me a knowing look.

Another French dinner, hmm? I nearly giggled, using my napkin to disguise it as a cough.

"This looks wonderful, Gladys. Thank you for including me," Griff started filling his plate, oblivious to our silent conversation.

"The Vegetable Tian looks especially gorgeous," I agreed. I heaped a pile of parmesan-covered, sliced eggplant, squash, tomato, and potato onto my plate. "You know, I believe this might be my first experience with tuna steak," I admitted.

"Really? How is that possible?" Sam asked as she spread her napkin daintily in her lap. "It's probably my favorite fish."

We munched quietly for several minutes, everyone enjoying the flavors and lost in their own thoughts.

"Well, I'm sold. The tuna is delicious Gladys." I cut a few more bites off of my fish.

"I agree. What did you use to make this great crust on the outside?" Sam asked before popping another piece into her mouth.

"Dried herbs and butter." Gladys scooped more veggies onto her own plate. "I'm glad that you like it. So, what's the plan?"

"Plan?" Sam asked.

"For figuring out who is trying to get to Piper."

"Wait a minute," Griff said. "These guys are dangerous. Nobody needs to do any figuring out. The sheriff was elected to do just that."

"Right you are!" Gladys smiled at Griff before sending a very obvious wink at Sam and I, nearly making me choke on my salad. "Griff, why don't you wait outside while the girls help me clear the table?" she asked not long after that, as the last fork clattered to its empty plate.

He frowned but wandered through the living room and out onto the back patio.

After the sliding door clicked shut, Gladys leaned forward and, with a conspiratorial whisper, said, "Okay, now tell me the truth. What are we going to do to get these people away from Piper? What do they want?"

Shrugging, I leaned my elbows on the table. "It has to be about the trial. That's the only thing that makes sense, yet at the same time, it makes no sense at all. Multiple people are supposed to testify, it isn't like things hinge on me alone to make charges stick to Regina."

"Plus, they have the voicemail on your phone. Isn't that going to be admitted into evidence? You shared it with Officer Grumpy over in Pierson County already," Sam ran her fingers through her long hair, making me wonder again exactly what *patriotic hair* would look like if the challenge were met and she dyed it for the holiday next month.

"Yes, I gave them the voicemail. Honestly, I have no idea what they think I can say in a trial that is going to be any different. I'm happy to leave it alone this time. Truly."

Sam and Gladys gave me skeptical looks. I shrugged and began picking up dishes, carrying them to the kitchen.

After cleaning the kitchen, at least partially before Gladys insisted that she could do it tomorrow, we joined Griff on the patio.

"How are Jack and Drew?" I asked after a lull in the conversation.

"Fairing pretty well," Gladys answered. "Though truth be known, Drew's been pouting about the heat wave."

Griff looked to me, confusion wrinkling his brow.

"You haven't met Jack and Drew, have you, Griff?"

"No, can't say that I have."

"Why, where are my manners!" Gladys stood and reached for Griff's hand. "I'll introduce you at once."

"Isn't it a bit late to be dropping in on people?" he reached to set down his glass of water before Gladys tugged him away from the patio table.

Sam bit her lip to stifle the laughter.

I did my best to remain expressionless, only offering a shrug when Griff looked to me to chime in.

A few quick steps down the stone path and Gladys halted in front of two palm trees, one tall

71

and the other short and stubby. "Here we are," she said. "This big fella is Jack. Drew is younger and still moody, but don't tell him I said so," Gladys whispered behind her hand.

Griff stared for a moment and leaned closer. I imagined the detailed facial features carved into the trees were slightly harder to make out in the dim evening light. After a moment though, he saw them. "I see what you mean there, about Drew pouting," Griff pointed. The smaller tree's leaves were drooping low, rather than fanning out. Sam and I held in a giggle as Gladys fawned over her creations with a new audience.

Shortly after Griff had the pleasure of meeting Jack and Drew, and once he had complimented Gladys on her woodcarving skills, we excused ourselves and the three of us headed to our vehicles.

"I'm going to follow you home and make sure you are safe in your apartment," Griff held the door of my truck open for me.

"Don't argue," Sam leaned out the window of her car as she backed down the drive. "He's following you or else." Sam simply smiled and waved as I stuck my tongue out at her. "Be safe," she called.

~

Pulling up into the dimly lit lot of my apartment complex, I scanned the dim parking lot. No white Mercedes. I exhaled and parked.

Griff pulled into the spot next to my truck. I stepped closer as he rolled down the passenger side window.

"Thanks for making sure I got home safely," I told him, standing on the running board to better see inside the cab.

"Always," he smiled. "Now, go get some rest. You'll need it. I plan to take you on our first date tomorrow night."

"Oh? But you haven't asked me," I waggled my eyebrows at him.

"That's because I don't care if I have to kidnap you myself, you're going."

I laughed. "How about I give in and say a date sounds lovely? It would be a fun new experience whereas the role of the kidnap victim is getting kind of old."

I headed inside, locking the door behind me. Though I was still stuffed from supper at Gladys's house, my sweet tooth was kicking in. From the cabinet in the kitchen, I took out my stash of dark chocolate chips, poured some into a small bowl, and carried them to my bedroom. I changed into comfy shorts and a t-shirt, emptying the pockets of my cargo pants before tossing all of the clothes into a heap in the bathroom floor. Laundry was a chore that could wait for tomorrow.

Plumping my pillows behind me, scooting my bowl of dark chocolate chips closer, I settled into my bed crossed-legged and opened the little notebook, deciding to get some work done on plans for the Fourth of July desserts.

Beep.

I checked my phone, expecting to see a message from Sam. It was Millie.

> Millie: Wanted to check in on you guys. Was everything okay this afternoon?

How sweet. I texted her back right away.

> Me: Thanks for asking! All is good now. See you tomorrow afternoon?

> Millie: Yep. Cya.

I took time to text Sam as well, knowing she would appreciate it.

> Me: Home safe. Planning red, white, and blue dessert menu. Ideas?

> Sam: Go. To. Bed.

> Me: So, no ideas?

> Sam: Strawberry. Blueberry.

Me: 😊 Great. Night.

I added some fruit-jelly sandwich cookies to the list, scribbling the last word with a yawn. Sam was right, as usual; I should sleep.

Taking my now empty bowl to the kitchen, I turned off lights and set the thermostat a little cooler. I hesitated before going back to the bedroom. Tiptoeing to my window, I pulled back the curtain an inch and peeked out.

I wasn't prepared for the sight that met my eyes. My heart skipped a beat.

Griff still sat in his truck, an eye on my place. My own personal guardian angel. I dropped the curtain before he noticed me.

Chapter 8

On Friday morning, Sam and I pulled into the parking lot of the bakery at nearly the same time.

I had slept like a baby, confident that Griff would keep me safe. I heard his truck rumble to life when I began clicking on lights this morning, and another peek through the window showed him driving away; he had stayed all night long.

"Morning," I cringed, hearing the chipper tones in my own voice.

Sure enough, Sam looked at me with suspicion. "Why do you sound so refreshed and eager to start the day?"

"Excited to be at work?" I tried.

"Not buying it," she unlocked the door and we went into the kitchen. Victoria and Millie wouldn't be coming in until after lunch. Gladys wasn't planning to work the register today, but I expected we would see her later in the morning regardless. For now, it was just the two of us.

"I don't know what you're talking about."

"You've never been able to keep secrets from me," Sam insisted. "Why think now is any different? I was up half the night worrying about you and here you are with a spring in your step as if nothing is wrong, no bad guys tried to get you, nobody put a tracker on your phone, all is right with the world."

"I'm sorry you didn't sleep well!" Guilt curled in my belly. Poor Sam, I didn't realize she had been so worried.

"Are you telling me you slept fine?"

I nodded. "Griff slept in his truck in the parking lot. I don't think he wanted me to know, so that's why I didn't say anything. If I had known how worried you were, I would have texted you."

"Sheesh. You owe me a nap," she fiddled with the Keurig until it lit up. Placing a large cup under the spicket, she put a dark roast coffee pod in and hit start.

"I can't do anything about naptime, but what if I tell you something else that will make you forget all about being tired and annoyed with me?"

"Fat chance," she crossed her arms. "But I guess I'll let you try." Sam's ever-present smile broke free. "Tell me what?"

"Griff and I have a date tonight."

"What?!" Her shriek filled the room. I hoped Flo wasn't next door yet, she'd certainly think one of us was getting murdered.

"Yep, attendance is apparently mandatory." I grinned, opening the large fridge door and retrieved two bowls of chilled cookie dough, closing the door with my foot.

"Well, it is about time." Sam picked up her coffee cup, add an ice cube, and placed it on the stainless-steel worktable. "Want me to get started on the unicorns?"

I chuckled. She wouldn't say I was right, of course, but I knew Sam's newfound energy had nothing to do with the coffee and everything to do with my news. Rather than find it odd, Sam had accepted the fact that her brother and I had feelings for each other, seemed delighted by it as a matter of fact.

"If you could handle the unicorns that would be awesome," I answered her.

An order for two dozen unicorn sugar cookies, complete with glitter decoration, had to be made this morning for a young woman to pick up before lunch. The woman, Mary, had volunteered to handle food for her niece's birthday party. "They have to be spectacular," she had told us. "I do have a reputation as the best aunt ever to uphold." We had laughed and promised to create majestic unicorn cookies.

A banging on the back door caused me to slip and cut my finger with the knife I'd been using to slice small rounds out of the cookie dough log in front of me.

"Who in the world could that be?" I wondered aloud as I wadded a paper towel onto my finger to staunch the bleeding.

We didn't have to wait long to find out.

"Piper, Sam. It's Flo." Bang. Bang. Bang. "Can you let me in?"

Sam unlocked the door and Flo slipped inside. Sam checked outside before shutting and locking the door again. "Flo, is everything okay?" she asked.

"It worked!"

"What worked?" I pulled the paper towel from my finger. Blood bubbled up and I put it back, surprised at how deeply I had cut it.

"The ad." Flo grabbed Sam by the hands and spun her in a circle. "The ad worked. There were three orders before I closed yesterday and another seven on the answering machine this morning."

"Congratulations!" Sam smiled.

"That's great," I added. Warmth bubbled up inside of me, a sense of pride that our idea was helping Flo's store.

"I better get started," Flo released Sam's hands. "I couldn't wait another minute to tell you and to thank you both. Piper, what happened to your finger?"

"Just an accident."

"You should really be more careful," Flo admonished as she left.

"I'm so happy business is picking up for her," Sam locked the back door for the umpteenth time that morning.

"Definitely." I washed and bandaged my finger before getting back to work.

~

Hours later, I placed the last tray of Strawberry Lemonade Cookies onto a rack to cool. Right now, they were simply strawberry sugar cookies; I would have to wait a while before being able to frost them with the lemon-infused frosting.

"Holy sprinkles! Sam those unicorns look magical."

"Do you think so?" she put down the piping bag and flexed her fingertips. "I've still got several more to go."

I stared at the platter containing the finished cookies. Whimsical, glittering masterpieces. The horn on each unicorn was silver sanding sugar, it might as well have been stardust. Long elegant necks and the head were white royal icing. Each unicorn had a swirling mane of pink, purple, and orange buttercream. Every one, that is, except a single unicorn cookie, on a plate of its own.

"What is that one?" I gestured to the cookie set apart.

Sam picked up the plate, bringing it closer for me to admire. This unicorn was a shimmering pink – royal icing sprinkled with pearlescent glitter – with a golden horn and deep violet buttercream mane. "This, this is the special cookie for the special birthday girl," Sam flashed a smile my way before putting the plate back down. "What do you think?"

"I think that Mary will forever hold the title of best aunt ever when she shows up to the party with these cookies." I dipped a finger in the bowl of leftover icing. "I better go unlock the doors. I'll be in the café if you need me."

Sam didn't answer, caught up in the tiny details of her creations once again.

Chapter 9

"Hey there," I greeted as Landon walked in the door midmorning. "I didn't know we would be seeing you today."

"Hey yourself," he said as he neared, leaning on the counter. "Is Sam here? I have a favor to ask the two of you."

"Sure, let me get her." I pushed open the swinging door and stuck my head in. "Sam, do you have a minute?"

"Be right there," she called.

"She'll be right out," I told Landon. "Can I get you anything? Cookie? Coffee?"

"Coffee and one of those fancy scone things would be great. I haven't eaten breakfast yet."

"Grab a table and I'll bring it over."

Landon nodded and chose a table in the corner, close to the counter.

"Hey, Piper what's up? Did you need me to watch the register?" Sam stopped as she noticed Landon, brushing strands of red and blonde hair behind her ear. "Hi, Landon."

Landon stood up, hugging Sam and pulling out a chair for her to be seated. I brought a plate of Nutella Scones to the table with a coffee for Landon and plenty of extra napkins. I watched the two of them chatting as I sat down, pulling out my own chair.

We each helped ourselves to a scone and, after a bite, I asked, "What's this favor you need?"

"Favor?" Sam echoed.

"Yes. If you can't help, it is no big deal, but I thought it would be worth asking." Landon wiped his hands on a napkin and took a drink of coffee. Our other patrons were settled in at their own tables, conversations humming all around. "Thanks to the arrests at the massage parlor in Lion's Cove, BeeBee was recognized as a victim and the police released her right away. That's the good news."

"There's bad news?" Sam leaned forward.

Nodding, Landon continued. "BeeBee has nowhere to go right now, no money to get her own place, and no job anymore."

"I thought Breaking Chains had rehabilitation programs and things like that?" I nibbled on another small bite of scone.

"We do. Unfortunately, BeeBee doesn't trust any of it. She's afraid she'll get swept off into another hell-hole somewhere and forced to do things she doesn't want to. She is determined to make a life for herself, which I understand, but you can see she has no idea where to start."

"That poor girl. What is the favor you need from us?" Sam asked.

"I think she would trust the two of you. Heck, I think she already does to a degree; she did talk to you, after all, and try to help when you were investigating to clear my name. I thought maybe you could brainstorm some ideas that would help her get back on her feet, reach out to her?" Landon ran his hands through his hair. "It's a lot to ask, and like I said…"

"We'd love to help," Sam put a hand on his arm and stopped him. "Isn't that right, Piper?"

"In any way we can," I agreed. My heart ached for BeeBee. The young Asian girl we met during our weekend trip to Lion's Cove had been scared, but strong. I couldn't imagine the things she had been through. I found myself eager to help her; to find out her story and help her write the rest of it herself.

"How do we reach her?" Sam, always a step ahead, wanted to know.

"I'm going to give her your numbers, put the choice in her hands."

"Start giving her control in her own life and choices again," I nodded. "Landon, that is so smart!" I stepped away for a moment as Mary came in to pick up the Unicorn Birthday Cookie order. She was thrilled, as predicted, and gave Sam a hug when I pointed her out as the decorator.

Closing up the cash register, I rejoined Sam and Landon at the table. Landon stood, getting ready to leave.

"Thank you," he said. "Thank you both. I'm going to go, we're still cleaning up Regina's mess at the office, but I'll get in touch with BeeBee right away. Hopefully, she will contact one of you soon."

Sam wiped down the table after Landon left. Gladys strolled in right after.

"I passed that cute boy, Landon." She carried a large paper sack with her. "Piper, tell me, was he here to try and wrestle you away from Griff?"

I laughed. "No. I do think he may be trying to steal a heart, but it isn't mine."

Gladys narrowed her eyes and glanced at Sam then back at me. "You don't say...interesting. I'm going to have to keep an eye on this."

Amused at how invested Gladys was in our lives, yet puzzled at why she would be keeping her cooking classes secret from us, I decided to change the subject. "What's in the bag?"

Sam finished cleaning the tables and joined us. "Hey, Gladys. What have you got there?"

"Supplies, my dears. Supplies. I was about to ask Piper if we might go in the back so I can show you." Gladys darted her eyes around.

Other than a group of ladies chatting and enjoying coffee, and their kids fighting over cookie pieces at the next table, the bakery had emptied out of customers.

"Let me top off these coffees and then I'll be back. You two go ahead," I motioned them ahead of me to the kitchen.

Not a minute later, the three of us sat at stools at the stainless-steel island.

"So, what are the supplies for?" I asked.

"Safety, of course."

Sam and I shared a concerned look.

"Whose safety?"

"Ours. While we figure out who is after you. Not to mention you seem to have a nasty habit of getting into tight spots."

I shrugged. Lately, she was correct.

Gladys unfolded the brown paper bag and reached a hand inside. "Now let's see here," she muttered. "Ah! There you are."

Out of the bag came an industrial sized can of pepper spray. Followed by two more.

"Gladys, really…" I began.

Sam snatched up one of the cans. "Awesome! I didn't know they came this big." She stuffed it in her purse. I glared. She shrugged. "Saved your butt with it yesterday, didn't I?"

I made a face and remained quiet.

Rustling noise drew our eyes back to Gladys. She was elbow deep into the bag again. *Seriously, there's more?* This time three tiny bottles appeared.

"Awe! What are those little things?" Sam's voice dripped with delight; she loved miniature things.

Gladys spun the bottles to face us.

"Amino Energy Plus," I read the label.

"Blue Raspberry flavor!" Sam sounded far too excited about everything in Gladys's bag of *supplies.*

"And we will need this because?"

"Piper, we need this on a regular day. Just think how much more we need it on a day when you've been being stubborn, kidnapped, attacked, or I've been awake worrying about you being stubborn, kidnapped, and attacked." Sam scooped up her energy drink and added it to her purse.

"Plus, I'm sure we might need it for some all-night stakeouts," Gladys clapped hopefully.

"Unlikely," I warned.

"Party pooper," she huffed.

Sandwich size Ziploc bags were added to the pile.

"Please explain." I crossed my arms.

"I'm lost on this one, too," Sam admitted.

"Girls, don't you know Ziploc bags can be used for almost anything?" She held up a hand and began ticking off a list on her fingers. "Collecting evidence. Carrying emergency cookies. Piping frosting. Microwaving omelets. Avoiding leaving fingerprints."

Sam snagged four or five bags and added them to her purse, her grin growing by the minute.

My jaw dropped. There wasn't even time for me to process the things wrong with that list before Gladys began searching the bag a fourth time. Sam and I waited in silence.

The voice of Dory shouting *Eh Mr. Grumpy Gills* made me jump and Gladys lunged for a can of pepper spray.

"Gladys, it's my phone," I held out my hands, motioning for her to stop.

"You have got to change that ringtone," Sam said. "It's dangerous."

I refused to admit it out loud, but she was right; that ringtone had a habit of going off at bad times and was the reason we got caught and held captive last weekend. I answered the phone, managing to swipe the screen before the call went to voicemail.

"Hello?"

"Piper Rivers?" the gravelly voice snapped.

"Yes, sir."

"This is Officer Campbell. It seems, well, it seems the voicemail you provided has been lost."

"Lost?"

"Lost. Erased. Stolen. Corrupted. Deleted. I don't really know; I don't understand all that technical mumbo-jumbo," Officer Campbell yelled through the phone. Quieting, he continued. "It's gone. We need that voicemail introduced during your testimony on Monday. Understood?"

"Yes, I understand." I nodded though he obviously couldn't see me. "I'll bring it. About Monday," I swallowed, my throat suddenly dryer than a bag of crushed graham crackers. "Monday, do you think the voicemail is enough? Maybe my testimony isn't really a big deal…."

"You will testify Monday, you have to." Officer Campbell hung up the phone.

"Well?" Sam tapped her fingers on the table and tilted her head.

"I think I know why someone doesn't want me to testify."

"Why?"

"The voicemail is gone. The file is gone or damaged, something that makes it unusable now. My testimony and my phone are the only records of Regina's confession to the arson and kidnapping."

"You know what that means," Gladys spoke up. We turned to look at her across the table. "It means we definitely needed my bag of supplies. Regina's thugs will keep coming for you."

"I really hope you're wrong," I told her.

"Still," Sam motioned to the bag. "Let's see the rest."

Gladys gleefully resumed her reveal of the supplies.

Next came three tiny plastic squares with a hole punched in them.

Sam raised an eyebrow.

"Key finders. I couldn't afford those fancy GPS secret spy locators. Besides," Gladys smiled, "these came in a three-pack so I took it as a sign."

Another hand went into the paper bag.

"What is this, Mary Poppins's magic paper sack?" I couldn't believe what I was seeing. Surely the bag should've burst with all the things it held inside.

Sam continued to stick goodies in her purse.

"Almost done," Gladys promised. "Here we are, my very favorite thing."

"Is that…," Sam wiggled around on her stool like a kid at Christmas.

"A panic button!" Gladys's eyes shone triumphantly, a glow of pride on her face.

I looked at the round red and silver objects, small enough to fit in the palm of my hand. "What do you do with a panic button?" I frowned.

Sam leaned across the table and tapped the red button. A shrill whistle pierced the air, followed by whirring sirens and something blathering on like Daffy Duck.

I covered my ears.

Gladys tapped the button again and the noises ceased.

Realizing we had been in the back far too long, and concerned our customers might be freaking out after the panic button alarms, I pushed through the swinging door to check things out.

One child was curled in his mother's lap crying. Two others were plastered to the front glass looking for police cars outside.

"I'm so sorry," I apologized as the women at the table looked up at me. "A friend, she was playing a prank. Can I get you a few more cookies, on the house?"

Once I had bagged up half a dozen Chocolate Chunkies and waved the ladies and kids out the door, I re-entered the kitchen.

Sam's purse now bulged at the seams. My set of supplies and Gladys's were still spread across the island.

"Where did you get all of this stuff anyway?" I asked picking up a panic button, careful not to press it.

"Amazon of course," Gladys said as if there weren't any other places to shop.

"I hate to break it to you," I crossed my arms, "but these things aren't all going to fit in my pockets. The one day I've carried a purse this month I was accosted and a phone planted on me, so I'm out on that option."

"Don't you think I thought of that?" Gladys asked.

"Um...I don't know. Did you?"

"Of course. I was just telling Sam that I have the perfect solution for you when she asked the same question."

"You were?" I looked at Sam. She studiously avoided eye contact. Not good.

"Yes. Here." Gladys turned the paper bag upside down. "You can even pick which color: camo or black."

I gaped. Sam had turned her back completely to us but I could see her shoulders shaking in silent laughter.

"I got myself one, too; purses get in the way if you need to run." Gladys held up the two plastic fanny packs. "What'll it be, black or camo?"

I groaned. "Black." I took the bag, cringing at the thought of putting the shiny plastic pouch around my waist, but knowing there was no getting out of it with these two. I stuffed the fanny pack full of the supplies. The buckle snapped into place with a loud click. I tried to adjust the pack so that it sat more toward my hip; maybe I could block people's view of it with my arm.

"Now we're ready." Gladys patted her own fanny pack, smack dab in the middle of her waist.

"For what?" I asked.

"For anything."

I seriously doubted that but was smart enough to maintain my silence.

Chapter 10

"Piper!" The bell tingling over the door was drowned out by Flo's excited yell as she entered the bakery later Friday afternoon. "I've had ten more red, white, and blue flower arrangements today."

"That's great!"

"No."

I frowned. "It isn't great?"

"No. Yes. Well, it would be if I had about six hands."

"Oh." I understood. There had been more than a few times at the beginning of the Ooey Gooey Goodness Bakery where Sam and I thought we would never get enough baking done. Things improved as we got into routines, and now with

Victoria and Millie helping part-time things were simple most days.

"I don't know what I'm going to do," Flo continued.

"Millie!"

"What?" Flo looked at me as if I'd lost my mind.

The bell jingled and in walked Millie, whom I'd seen parking her scooter out front.

"You should ask Millie to help you, Flo. She's very artistic already, so you could probably teach her some tricks for flower arranging in no time."

"Did I hear my name?" Millie worked to smooth down strands of blonde hair that had been mussed up beneath her helmet.

Flo smiled. "Do you like flowers?"

Soon, it was settled. Millie would spend her afternoons working with Flo instead of at the bakery for the same amount of pay.

"This should be really fun! My art so far has all been two-dimensional." Millie chatted eagerly, asking questions and nodding as Flo answered. They set off for the flower shop to get started at once.

~

"You should go."

"Are you sure?" I asked Sam. The clock on the wall showed it was only a little after five that evening.

"Yes. Go. Relax, freshen up, get ready for your date." She shooed me away from the counter with a kitchen towel. "Victoria and I will manage everything fine until closing. She's back there whipping up some outrageous brownie batter as we speak."

Sam was right. They could handle things, even though it had been a busy afternoon. A lot of the customers coming in were placing advance orders for the Fourth of July with their coupons. It would be all-hands-on-deck next week for getting the extra orders ready.

"Thank you! I'll see you in the morning." I hugged Sam and stepped through the swinging door to the kitchen. Delicious chocolate aromas filled the room and I stopped to enjoy them for a moment. After telling Victoria goodbye, and swiping a finger through the bowl of brownie batter for tasting, I traded my apron for my keys and headed to my truck.

Outside the sun still shone brightly and the heat evoked immediate drops of sweat on my neck and forehead. I wiped them off, getting into and cranking the truck. As I leaned forward to set the

AC temperature cooler, I noticed a fluttering through the windshield; a yellow paper was stuck below the truck's windshield wiper. I opened the door and stood, leaning out and snatching the paper inside the truck with me before slamming the door back.

"What have we here?" I mused. The yellow paper was lined, appearing to be a standard sheet torn from a notepad, and folded into a small rectangle. I unfolded the paper. A note, handwritten in large letters, said: **MEET ME. 113 CRESTWAY. RIGHT AWAY.**

I turned the paper over. No signature. I pulled out my phone and saw one missed call from Griff. Griff! I put the truck in drive. Maybe this was his way of being romantic. I did think our date was supposed to be later this evening, but I wouldn't put it past him to try and surprise me. I drove toward Crestway street, smiling as I tried to figure out where we might be going over there.

The address wasn't far away. It was in a newer part of town. So new, in fact, that when I pulled up at what the GPS said was number 113, I realized there wasn't even a completed building here; it was a construction site. *Maybe Griff had to work late on an inspection* I decided *and he didn't want to cancel our date.*

I parked on the street and hopped out of the truck. Beeping the lock button, I started walking toward the open gate in the chain link fence surrounding the property. When I didn't see Griff's truck after walking several yards onto the site, an uneasy feeling began creeping up my spine and along my neck. I continued walking as I dialed Griff's cell. The ringing went unanswered, voicemail picking up. I hung up the phone, deciding I would have to text him instead.

A noise past the dumpster and by a stack of pallets captured my attention. It sounded male, maybe someone talking on the phone. I relaxed, rolling my shoulders to loosen the tension that had been building. If Griff were on the phone with a client, he wouldn't be able to take my call. I walked slowly in the direction of the voice, not wanting to interrupt.

Oh sheesh, the fanny pack I palmed my forehead, embarrassed, chiding myself for not taking the silly thing off as soon as Gladys left the bakery. I started to unbuckle it -at least if I carried it, it wouldn't look as much like I was a tourist on vacation for the first time ever – but left it on. If I was carrying it around that would look even stranger. Griff would be sure to ask what was inside, and I didn't want to have to tell him about Gladys's supplies.

As I got closer, the voice carrying to me rose and I realized two things: one, that wasn't Griff; two, whoever it was sounded angry.

Chapter 11

I froze. Now that I was closer, I could hear a second voice. This one was lower and talking fast; too fast, the words were impossible to make out. Griff wasn't here. I was certain of that now. I began to tiptoe backward.

A sharp noise cracked like thunder in the quiet evening, then a second, both echoing off of the large metal dumpster.

A yelp escaped me, the noise catching me completely off guard.

A thud followed, like that of dropping something heavy on the ground, and then the loud, angry voice shouted. "Who's there?"

I turned tail to run, but it was too late.

"Stop!"

Regretting it, but too scared to disobey, I stopped and turned back to the source of the noise. Sure enough, the man who had stepped out from his place of cover was holding a shiny black gun. *Gulp.* Aimed right at me.

"Toss the phone." Covered in tattoos from his neck down to his wrists, he stared at me with cold eyes. Not a muscle twitched, there was no falter, his arm perfectly steady as the gun remained leveled at my chest.

I tossed my phone, throwing it a couple of feet to my right. No way was I putting it closer to him than to me. It began to ring. Of course! Now that I couldn't possibly answer and scream for help.

A sharp crack reverberated through the air.

My eyes squeezed shut reflexively, waiting for the impact. Nothing. No pain. No other sounds. Forcing my eyes open one at a time, I risked a look at the man. Chills racked my body when I saw a malicious smile. I forced myself to look away, to follow the new direction of the gun barrel.

My phone lay dead in the dirt. Murdered. Shot in the back.

I looked back to find the smile gone, replaced by a sneer more suited to his face. One shot, perfect aim, no mistakes – those were the things I knew he was communicating to me. I forced myself to control the shaking, to swallow the bile rising up my throat.

"Looks like it's just the two of us now." His words confirmed my fears. The other man I had heard was already dead. I might be next.

"Come over here. I have something to show you," he gestured with the gun, ensuring it was never pointed far off me as I edged nearer. He kept me walking, forcing me around the pallets. My knees turned to jelly and I dropped to the ground. Staring down into a large hole, I saw the body of the man who attacked me in the bakery.

"This is what happens to associates of mine who fail. Though in the end, I guess he did get you here. Oh well." There wasn't a trace of guilt or regret in his voice, only amusement. After a moment he added, "This is also what happens to the meddling woman who got my son arrested."

Uh-oh. I couldn't quite fathom this man being Asnee's father; he looked young enough to be the same age. Now wasn't the time to demand a look at the family tree, though. I had to think of a way out of here. Nobody even knew where I was!

I looked around at the gaping hole in the earth, the crumpled man at the bottom of it, and the giant pile of dirt beside it. The shovel standing stoically nearby, ready to be used, pushed me over the edge, almost literally. My stomach couldn't handle anymore. I twisted around and threw up. As my bad luck would have it, I tossed my cookies right on the gunman's shoes.

"Why you disgusting..." spewing what I assumed were obscenities and curses in another language, the man lashed out with a swift kick. His booted foot caught me in my now empty stomach, launching me into the makeshift grave. I landed hard, knocking the wind from my lungs. I gasped and heaved in great gulps of air. Tears were starting to well up, whether from pain, fear, or lack of breath I had no idea. I racked my brain. The hole was deep. It must have been dug for a well or a septic tank; regardless, there was no climbing out fast enough to avoid being shot.

I couldn't panic.

Panic! Panic, that's it!

I unzipped the fanny pack, praising it as the best accessory ever known to man, and grabbed the panic button, dropping it in my hurry. Thank God the man must still be busy rubbing vomit off his shoes or I'd probably be dead by now. I grabbed it from the dirt, doing my best to ignore the stiff arm it had landed next to, and prayed that Gladys had been thoughtful enough to put batteries in them. I squeezed the little button for all I was worth and resisted the urge to cover my ears when wailing and sirens erupted.

Above me, more cursing ensued. A shadow fell over me and I saw the gun pointed my direction. I dove as several shots fired in my direction. Burning seared my shoulder and several more rounds thudded into the dirt wall. I didn't move for several minutes; playing dead worked for opossums and I wasn't above trying it. I maintained a rigid grasp on the panic button in my hand, the noise so close to my ear I feared I might be deaf if I somehow made it out of here alive. *Alive – oh no, what if he buries me alive.* Great, now that thought embedded itself in my head, I didn't know what would be worse, getting shot and buried, or not getting shot and still getting buried.

When no more gunshots came, and no shovels full of dirt plopped onto my head, I ventured a peek up to the surface of the hole. Seeing nobody, I unclenched my fingers from around the panic button. The ringing continued in my ears at least sixty seconds afterward, but eventually, silence trickled back around me. Carefully, I uncurled and stood up.

Pain shot through my left arm as I lifted them both and tried to jump up. As suspected, I could get nowhere near the top. Turning my attention to my left arm, I lifted the now torn sleeve of my t-shirt. A deep gouge to the outside of my shoulder had blood trickling slowly down my arm. Somewhere in the back of my head, I heard myself thinking this must be what they call a flesh wound, and then I threw up again.

Pulling myself together, I put the panic button back in the fanny pack. I pulled out the little-bitty energy drink bottle and chugged it. Now that I was done freaking out, I had to get out of this hole.

Chapter 12

"No, not again! Please!" I landed on my feet in the bottom of the hole as yet another root I'd been using as a handhold tugged loose, oblivious to my pleading, and sent me flying.

Digging the toes of my sneakers into the crevices I had dug out about a foot up from the floor, I began again. Scrabbling for holds in the dirt, thick roots, anything I could find, I began my slow and painful ascent. My shoulder throbbed. My fingernails hurt from having dirt shoved up beneath them further and further. And the stench in this hole was unbearable. Thank goodness this pit was wide enough to keep me from falling on top of the body; I'm not sure I could have handled that.

I jerked to a stop when the sound of more than dirt falling around me caught my ear. An engine! Someone was driving around up at the construction site. Car doors slammed and I caught my breath. Sweat ran down my back, tickling, urging me to move, but I kept as rigid as possible. *Do I call out? Or stay silent? Are they friend? Or foe?* My thoughts rattled back and forth; an impossible decision that could have dangerous consequences.

Beeeeeeep-beeeeeeep-beeeeep! The high-pitched sound in my fanny pack made me jump. *What in the world is that?* Different than the panic button, it was still loud. I cringed, digging around in my pack. Any chance I had at a cover was blown now.

I heard muffled voices and shoes shuffling on dirt. Seconds later, three heads peeked over the edge of my prison.

"Thank God!" I exclaimed at the sight of Griff, Sam, and Gladys.

Griff disappeared and reappeared with a long length of chain from somewhere nearby. "Grab onto this," he said, lowering the chain down next to me a little at a time.

Gingerly, bracing myself for another fall, I transferred my hands from the root I clung to, over to the chain. With a firm grip, I nodded at Griff and walked my feet up the wall as my friends pulled the chain. Once I was a few feet from the top, Griff handed the chain over to Gladys and Sam. He dropped down on his stomach, grabbing my hands and pulling me the rest of the way out. Carefully, I pulled myself into a sitting position on the ground.

"Ahh-ouch!" I cried out as Sam wrapped me in a bear hug.

"What's wrong?" she pulled back.

"Are you okay?" Griff knelt down beside me.

Beeeeeeep-beeeeeeep-beeeeep. The shrill sound made us all jump.

"Sorry. Sorry!" Gladys fumbled with her phone as Griff and Sam shot annoyed looks her direction.

"What was that?" I asked.

Waving her cell phone, Gladys answered, "The key finder! That's how we found you. See, I knew it would be perfect. A little dot shows up on my phone when I searched your key fob and then we came here but only saw your truck so I hit the alert button and voila, there you were."

"Gladys, I think I could kiss you right now! Your pack saved me more than once today."

"No thanks, Piper, but if that cute boyfriend of yours is feeling generous," she said, winking at Griff.

I think I saw him shuffle closer to the hole I'd just climbed out of.

Gladys waved her arms toward the hole. "Do you think we need to get that other guy out?" She leaned toward the edge.

Sticking my good arm out to stop her, I shook my head. "No. He's dead. We need to call Sheriff Kent."

Sam began dialing immediately while Griff helped me to my feet.

I winced. "Do any of you have a bottle of water?" I asked.

Gladys whisked a short, stubby water bottle from her fanny pack. "Here you go," she handed it to me.

I raised my eyebrows, beginning to wonder if we were back to Mary Poppins's carpet bag again.

"I thought of these for the supplies later on," she shrugged. "I didn't have time to add them to your pack or Sam's purse because you were already gone."

I took a swig of the lukewarm water. Then another, swishing it around to rinse my mouth. At last, I rolled up my sleeve again and poured a little on my shoulder. I tried to wipe the crusted blood and dirt away, but everywhere around it was so tender that tears sprang to my eyes.

"What is that?" Griff leaned closer to get a look at the angry, torn skin. "Piper! What happened?"

I quirked my mouth and shrugged my shoulders, trying to downplay the words as I uttered, "I got shot, but just a little."

"What?" Sam shrieked, before hurriedly assuring the sheriff that yes, we were all still fine. She updated him on my status, apologizing for screaming. "I'm sorry," she said into the phone. "I have to go; you have the address. Please get here soon. Thanks."

Griff's jaw was working overtime, clenching and unclenching. I could see the struggle between freaking out about my safety and trying to remain calm about the situation, physically battling for control. I reached up and put my right hand on his chest. "Hey," I said drawing his eyes to mine and away from my shoulder. "I'm fine. I'm okay." When he didn't relax, I poked him, hard. "I'm also hungry, and you owe me dinner."

"You're right about that. As soon as the sheriff clears us to leave, I'll take you to Sam's to get cleaned up and cook you a fantastic dinner myself. How's that sound?"

I pursed my lips. "That sounds like you are trying to manipulate me into spending the evening at your sister's instead of going home by myself." He started to protest but I held up a hand. "It also sounds delicious and like a fantastic plan," I smiled.

Gladys squealed, actually squealed like a little girl, buzzing with excitement as she caught up to the conversation. "You mean you two finally have a date? I knew it, I knew it. I told you, Piper, I knew he was boyfriend material the first day I saw you two together."

"Excuse me," Sam scowled, her usual smile having taken a hike somewhere far away. "Let's go back to the part, oh friend of mine, where you said you 'got a little shot'; you don't get a 'little' shot." She emphasized the word little with angry, jerking air quotes. "You either get shot or you don't. Why the heck did you not tell us right away that you were shot?" She fisted her hands on her hips.

Gladys, I noticed, was still holding up her phone doing something. Looking back at Sam, I said "This," and waved my hand in circles encompassing her from head to toe. "This crazy worried freak-out is why I didn't tell you. It barely grazed me, I'm fine, and you all get to say you saved the day so I don't know what the big deal is."

"Friends tell friends if they've been shot," she pouted.

I giggled.

She glared and I only giggled more. Maybe it was the shock, the hunger, the blazing heat, who knows. The statement echoed in my head and laughter was my only response. "I didn't read that in the manual," I told her. "Was it before or after friends don't get friends kidnapped?"

By the look on her face, I thought I might have to institute the rule that 'friends don't shoot friends', but thankfully was saved by the sound of sirens. Real sirens. "That reminds me," I turned to Gladys. "My panic button might need new batteries soon."

"Your what?" Griff narrowed his eyes. The three of us busted up laughing and his frown deepened. We were going to be in so much trouble.

Chapter 13

After relaying my statement to the sheriff, multiple times, he allowed me to leave on the condition that someone take me to the hospital to get checked out. My protests were ignored as I was bundled into Griff's truck and handed more water.

Now we finally arrived, two hours and three stitches later, at Sam and Griff's duplex. Gladys had gone home after we dropped her off at her car at the bakery.

"I think I should just go get in the ocean." The salty scent did more to relax me than anything else had all afternoon. "Who needs a shower anyway?" My rhetorical question earned me a few extra frowns.

"You can see the ocean later. You cannot sit on my furniture after sharing a room with a corpse," Sam crossed her arms.

"And I will not feed you if you do not shower," Griff added with a wink as he left us to go to his half of the duplex and prep supper.

"You two stink," I pouted.

"Nope," Sam laughed. "That's still you."

I trudged up the porch stairs after her and took myself straight to the shower. After a good sniff, I had to admit, she had a point.

The warm water was a welcome relief to my tight muscles. I had a bad feeling that tomorrow I would be sorer than I cared to think about. I scrubbed carefully around my stitches, gritting my teeth at the tenderness. By the time I got done showering, I couldn't decide which was worse: the pain from washing my hair, or the awkwardness of trying to wash it one handed when I gave up using both.

I dressed in a pair of Sam's yoga pants and a tank top, not exactly my first date outfit of choice, and brushed my teeth with the spare toothbrush I kept in Sam's guest bathroom. Looking in the mirror, I could see that the redness around my stitches had already started to go down. I braided my hair, gave myself one last glance, and went out to find Sam and Griff.

Searching Sam's side turned up nothing, but I heard voices coming from the big wraparound deck. I slid the glass door open and sure enough, there they both were over on Griff's side. He had the grill fired up and sizzling, smoky smells of beef beckoned me to join them pronto.

"What's cooking?" I asked as I slid into the chair next to Sam and accepted bottled water from the cooler. Beads of condensation sprung to life right away. It had to be ninety degrees out still, and that was with the breeze and the beginning of sunset.

Griff opened the grill to reveal thick, juicy New York strip steaks, corn on the cob, and a couple of foil packets containing something. "I hope you're still hungry," Griff said as he stuck the meat thermometer into one of the steaks.

"Famished," I assured him. My stomach growled in agreement. I didn't have to wait long. Griff began plating up the food minutes later, handing me a knife to cut the kernels of corn off the cob like he'd seen me do a million times.

As Griff sat the plates on the table, Sam reached carefully into the cooler and pulled out jugs of tea one at a time, unsweet for the two of us and sweet for Griff, and poured into the waiting glasses.

The foil packages were opened, releasing steam and more delicious aromas. One held buttery asparagus, another a garlic cauliflower and potato hash, and the last one brimmed with apple slices coated in cinnamon and brown sugar.

I munched happily on all of the delicious food and considered once again how blessed I was, not only to be alive but for this to be my life: amazing people who loved me and looked out for me, God's beautiful creation surrounding us to enjoy and never lacking for a meal.

"Well," Griff finished eating first and leaned back into his chair. "I called Sheriff Kent and, so far, he hasn't been able to come up with a name for the murdered man or the guy who claimed to be Asnee's father. He liaised with the officer in charge over in Pierson county. Said there was no record of Asnee when he was arrested, and the working theory is that most likely all of them are in the country illegally.

Disappointed, I only nodded and forked another bite of potatoes and cauliflower into my mouth.

Ding.

Sam looked down at her phone as it chimed again. Then she put down her fork and swiped it open. "It's BeeBee!"

"Really? What did she say?" I leaned over to read her screen. I'm sure we could add 'there's no such thing as privacy between friends' to the list of rules we'd been accumulating today; but truly, we had been friends too long to care. We shared everything and most people around us knew it. Heck, even Griff chose to get Gladys involved in sending a gift to me at the spa a few weeks ago because he knew Sam would tell me about it and spoil the surprise.

"She wants to meet us tomorrow."

"Okay."

"In Lion's Cove. She doesn't have a car or a way to get here," Sam continued to read. "She says she understands if we don't have time."

I licked my lips, thinking. "What do we have tomorrow?"

"That Girl Scout order," Sam reminded me.

"That's right," I snapped my fingers. "Trail Mix Cookie Cups for the Girl Scout birthday party. If we get those finished between nine and ten, we could head over and meet BeeBee for lunch."

"Victoria and Millie were planning to come in tomorrow anyway," Sam nodded. Her fingers whizzed over the touchscreen keyboard on her phone. "I'll ask Gladys to come too since Millie might still be helping Flo with flower arrangements."

"I guess that means no lunch date for you and me tomorrow," Griff said, having been quiet as we settled our plans.

My excitement about helping BeeBee dimmed somewhat. I wasn't used to planning around other people, and tonight's date already hadn't worked out the way either of us pictured.

"Tomorrow night?" I asked with a sheepish grin. Relief flooded me when he smiled.

"Sounds great," he reached over and squeezed my hand. "Why don't you two call it a night and I'll clean up out here?"

My answer was stolen by a great big yawn. I stretched and covered my mouth. Exhaustion was finally making an appearance. We agreed with Griff, though we did grab the paper plates to toss into the garbage, and headed back into Sam's side of the duplex to get some sleep.

Easier said than done.

Chapter 14

Slam! Clank, clank, clank.

I jerked to a sitting position in bed, still forcing my eyes open. The feel of a cold gun, the smell of death, my nightmares had been full of unsettling people and events; just snippets, scaring me awake and then fading away only to wake me in a cold sweat again an hour later.

Slam! The loud noise most recently responsible for waking me up sounded loudly again, assuring me it was not part of another nightmare.

"We're late!" Sam yelled from the hallway.

I rubbed more sleep from my eyes, cringing at the protest from my shoulder muscles. One Saturday morning, I need to make sleeping in an actual goal. Leaning gingerly over to the nightstand, I saw that my new phone was dead; we had bought it after leaving the hospital, but I'd forgotten to plug it in last night. With no other clock in the guest bedroom, there wasn't any other way to tell what time it was. Well, maybe there was one.

"Oh no," I groaned as I lifted the curtain and peeked out the window. Already light tinges of pink and purple were visible on the horizon. A beautiful sunrise meant we were very, very late.

I hurried to brush my teeth, bound my hair up in a wild bun and tied a bandana on like a headband to catch all of the loose tendrils. My cargo pants from yesterday were laying on the floor so I scooped them up and stepped into them, followed by a fresh t-shirt.

I stepped into the hall and was nearly trampled by Sam in a barefoot dash back to her room. "Tea is in the kitchen," she called.

Adding a few more ice cubes to my glass, I gulped the dark breakfast tea. The first drink after a mouth full of toothpaste was never pleasant, but once that taste dissipated, I slowed down and sipped a few more drinks.

"' K, I'm ready," Sam sped back into the room.

You would think that after a while I would no longer be amazed at my friend's ability to go from frazzled to foxy in under fifteen minutes. Nope. I stared at her, or maybe I glared but we were running late so who can say, and felt the familiar sense of awe come over me. A dark blue jumpsuit, speckled with white daisies, the hem barely skimming the tops of white wedge sandals at least four inches high. Silky strands of hair fell to her shoulder blades, all shiny and perfectly in place.

"You know," I said, as we hurried down the steps to her car and I marveled that she didn't break a leg in those shoes, "maybe Deidra was right. Maybe you shouldn't have gone into baking with me."

Sam shot me a puzzled frown.

"Did you ever consider fashion?" I asked her.

"Nah," she waved off the suggestion. "People are too picky, and commercial fashion is a joke. Can't you imagine how annoying it would be to work with some pretentious model who thought feathers and packing peanuts would make the ideal hat?"

I laughed; the flagrant image too easy to picture considering the ghastly displays on the runway of most designers these days.

The drive to work flew by. Flour coated our hands in no time as we baked at warp speed and prayed that we could catch up before time to open the bakery.

Tap tap tap. A light knock on the back door at six-thirty on the dot signaled that Victoria had arrived.

"Morning," I greeted as I unlocked the door to let her in.

"Hey!" She tied on an apron and stopped at the sink to wash her hands. "Where do you want me to start?"

~

It was a miracle. Between the three of us, the display case was fully stocked by the time we unlocked the door. I flipped the closed sign to the side reading 'Open for Ooey Gooey Deliciousness' and smiled. The sun was cresting the tops of the buildings on the other side of the street. All signs of purple were gone; the beautiful display now shot forth rays of deeper pinks lining the clouds and brilliant orange and yellow rays stretching across the sky.

"Good morning," I opened the door wide as a couple of men and women trickled in on their way to work to get a treat to take to the office with them.

After a few pleasant exchanges, and have a great day wishes, I watched the first group leave. Millie entered the front door, the bell jingling overhead.

"Morning," she bobbed her head, ponytail swinging merrily. "I told Flo that I would help her out until you and Sam are ready to leave."

"Thank you. Hey, how is flower arranging going anyway?"

"Not bad. I've decided I still like painting best, but there is some satisfaction in getting particularly stubborn flowers to do what you want. I have to admit; I never knew there were so many blue flowers in my life."

"I never thought of it like that, but I bet with Fourth of July arrangements you are seeing more than the usual number of blue flowers." I filled a to-go bag with Flo's normal scones plus a few extra goodies. "I'm going to have to stop by and see some of these arrangements obviously."

"Come get me when you and Sam need to leave; you can see them then," Millie waved and headed next door to Flo's Flowers.

I walked to the open pantry door where Sam counted ingredients for inventory.

"Are we going to need to pick up anything on our way back from Lion's Cove?" I asked as she scribbled on her clipboard.

"Definitely." More scribbling. "We are almost out of all the nuts, plus we are really low on baking chips."

"Yikes."

The bell above the door sounded. "Gladys is here," I told Sam before I walked over to greet our friend.

"Am I late?" she asked right away.

"No, you aren't late at all. In fact, you're earlier than expected. Are you okay? You look a little flushed."

"Pfft," she waved away my concern. "I'm fine. I had an appointment scheduled this morning that I'd forgotten about with all of the excitement yesterday."

Excitement? I didn't recall anything about my near-death experience or the friendly neighborhood corpse being exciting.

"How is your arm today?" Gladys asked.

"It's much better. Still sore but the longer I've been working it today, the better it seems to have gotten." I lifted my sleeve and we both looked at my stitches. I was happy to see no lingering redness. "Thanks for asking," I said as the sleeve dropped back into place. "Do you want a muffin this morning?"

"No, no." Gladys rubbed her stomach right above the camo fanny pack. "I've already eaten, but thanks. I should probably stock up on emergency cookies though." She began rummaging in the fanny pack, retrieving an empty Ziploc bag.

"Sam," I said as I noticed her coming toward us. "Did you hear that?"

"Hear what?"

"Gladys declined muffins."

As I knew it would, one delicate eyebrow raised in question and she looked from me to Gladys. "Are you sick?" Sam asked.

"No," Gladys put her hands on her hips.

Sam matched her, pose for pose. "Spill. Did you have another cooking lesson with Chef Fabio today?"

Gladys turned almost as purple as a grape. Her eyes widened and she started sputtering.

"It's okay," Sam soothed. "There's nothing to be ashamed of for taking a cooking class."

"That's right. I bet we would have fun in a baking class even," I added motioning to Sam and myself.

"I am *not* taking cooking lessons," Gladys dropped her arms to her side and stomped a foot.

"Millie spilled the beans," I said.

"That's right. The jig is up," Sam spread her arms out. "Why did you want to keep it a secret from us anyway?"

Grandpa Rex chose that moment to stroll into the bakery, his grandson little Tommy or little Timmy, I never could keep the twins straight, tagging along beside him. Gladys smiled and said hi, made polite conversation and then excused herself to the kitchen.

Left without much choice, Sam and I helped Grandpa Rex and his grandson pick out some treats for the weekend. Sam filled the coffee cup of a young woman reading at a back table. At last, we finished up and let the woman know she could ring the bell on the counter if she needed anything. We stepped into the kitchen to find Victoria handing Gladys a mug of coffee.

"Victoria," I looked around, ensuring oven timers were set and dishes were drying beside the sink. "Do you want to give the counter a try for a couple of minutes while we talk to Gladys?"

Surprise flitted across her face, her mouth forming a tiny O, but she wiped her hands and moved to the door. "No problem. You'll watch the cookies?" she asked.

I smiled, pleased to have such a conscientious helper. "Yes, I will get them out and onto cooling racks."

Victoria nodded and the door swung closed behind her.

"Gladys," I touched a hand to her shoulder, pulling up the stool next to her. "What's going on? You know you can tell Sam and me."

"Fine." She took a drink of coffee and wiped her mouth. "Are there any cookies in here?"

I smirked. *So much for not being hungry.*

Sam put three Peanut Butter M&M cookies on a napkin and put them between us. We sat in silence, letting the ooey gooey melted candies and heavy peanut butter taste mellow everyone out for a moment.

At last, Gladys put down the other half of her cookie and clasped her hands together. "First," she said sternly, leveling a great mom look on each of us, "I am not taking cooking classes."

We kept quiet, waiting for Gladys to go on.

She did. "I am Frédéric's assistant in the cooking classes at the Senior Citizen Center."

"Frédéric?" We both asked.

Gladys unclasped her hands and picked her cookie up again. "Yes, that is Chef Fabio's real name, known only to close friends." And with that she munched happily on her cookie, refusing to acknowledge the looks of shock and confusion on our faces. At least Sam's face was shocked and confused; I could only assume my expression was the same considering I didn't even know where to start with this new information.

Gladys, the personal assistant, or I suppose you would call that a sous-chef, to the French Chef Fabio. Eh, I shrugged mentally; I guess I'd heard of stranger things.

Buzzzzz!

"Alrighty then," I stood to turn off the oven timer. "Good for you."

"That's it?" Sam asked. "What aren't you saying, Gladys?"

Sliding some cute dolphin oven mitts off of the pegs and onto my hands, I removed first one and then the second sheet tray of cookies. I slid the parchment paper smoothly onto the cooling rack, a skill I never stopped being proud of when I thought back to the dozens of mangled cookies in my past before I learned to do it quickly enough.

"Frédéric and I are seeing each other," Gladys said. "Discreetly," she added as Sam and I both smiled. Sam began clapping her hands.

"How in the world did this happen?" I asked.

With a shrug, like it was no big deal at all, Gladys explained that she had seen Chef Fabio's name on the roster of classes offered and it had an email to RSVP for a spot, which was apparently limited.

"I told him I had taken his class before, at the O Heavenly Day Spa, and was very impressed. I asked if I might come to the class just to watch, I already know how to cook of course, and he offered to teach me some new French cooking styles if I would agree to assist instead of being a student."

"That explains the cooking classes part," Sam prodded, "but not the seeing each other part."

"Well, after the first few lessons, we realized we really enjoyed the company." Gladys blushed. "He's only eight years younger than me, though you wouldn't know it to look at him. Plus, girls, do you know how sexy a man who cooks is?"

I nodded. I did. Oh, I totally did.

She laughed as she said, "I loved my Harold; I still miss him, too, but that man couldn't boil water without nearly catching the house on fire."

I chuckled.

"Well," Sam patted Gladys's arm. "I think it's great. You shouldn't have to be lonely all of the time."

"I don't have time to be lonely anymore, not after meeting you girls."

135

I gave Gladys a hug, then moved to the racks of cooling cookies. "Sam, I'll take these out to stock the display. Do you think you can fill the cookie cups with the trail mix?" I took a look at my watch. "The Girl Scout troop leader should be here in half an hour to pick them up." Chocolate chip cookies molded around mini muffin pans and baked created the perfect little bowl to fill with treats, in this case, the trail mix filling would have M&Ms, coconut, pretzel pieces, and raisins. They were going to be adorable and functional little desserts.

"I've got it," Sam shooed me out of the kitchen.

Not long after the troop leader picked up the three dozen Trail Mix Cookie Cups, we were in Sam's car and headed to Lion's Cove.

"Will you text BeeBee and let her know we should arrive by eleven?" Sam handed me her cell phone.

I sent the message and waited for a response. "BeeBee says to meet her at the fast-food place on the left right as we get to town; it's called Chicken Shack." I eased Sam's phone back into the holster on the dash. She clicked the button for navigation and put in our updated destination.

We drove for a time with the windows down and the radio cranked up. After about an hour, Sam pulled into a Sonic drive-thru and ordered us a couple of limeades. I had a Blue Raspberry Limeade while Sam chose a Frozen Strawberry Limeade.

Instead of turning the radio back up, when she merged onto the highway Sam asked, "Have you tried to prepare for Monday yet?"

"Monday?" I tilted my head as I took another delicious sip of cold, fizzy limeade.

"Yes, Monday. You know – court, trial, testifying, maybe not passing out. That Monday. The day after tomorrow, Monday."

"Okay, I get it. Sheesh."

"Well then?"

Slurp.

"Piper!"

Slurp.

"Seriously right now?"

"Fine. I haven't figured out what I'm going to do." I put my foam cup into the cupholder and worried my hands together, rubbing my fingers and wrists. "Obviously, I can't just not testify. I could get arrested or fined or whatever the penalty is for failure to appear, withholding evidence, and whatever other legal sounding things they can put on me, since the fear of public speaking isn't exactly punishable."

"Wow."

"Hey, you asked." I crossed my arms, then changed my mind and picked up my drink. I resumed my slurping, loud and obnoxious slurping.

"Maybe all you need is a little practice," Sam told me.

Slurp. "What kind of practice?" Slurp.

"You know, talking in front of a few groups of people. Maybe you could make an announcement on tonight's news broadcast advertising the promo sale between Ooey Gooey Bakery and Flo's Flowers?"

"Ha. There's no way to get on the news without setting it up further in advance than a couple of hours."

Slurp. Slurp. Slurp. This time, Sam became very consumed with her drink and the road in front of us.

I knocked her hand away as she reached for the volume knob on the radio. "Samantha Lowe. What. Did. You. Do." I used my best stern voice. A headache began in the base of my skull, and I was certain the limeade hadn't caused it.

"I may have already scheduled a slot. Missy will be by the bakery at seven tonight to air it live on the late news." Missy was our local news channel's main reporter. She had been by the bakery only one other time and that was also for a short interview.

"You're kidding me." My glare was useless as she kept her eyes glued to the road.

"'Fraid not," she said.

I took another long pull from my straw but sucked up nothing but air thanks to my continual slurping earlier. Great.

"I don't like you," I told Sam.

"I know," she shrugged and a hint of a smile turned the corner of her mouth up as she reached for the radio again. "You have to be ready for Monday though."

As I grumbled about busybodies, horrible friends, and general rudeness, Sam continued to increase the volume. Laughter bubbled from her lips and soon I gave up and stared silently out of the window. I would get out of it, somehow, then Sam could do the interview herself. Now, to think of a plan.

We arrived at Chicken Shack at five after one. I still had no idea what I would do to extricate myself from tonight's interview. With a sigh, I got out and slammed the door of the car.

"There's BeeBee," Sam tugged at my arm, making me wince. "Oops, sorry."

BeeBee stood up from the gray bench by the door when we approached. "Thanks for coming," she kept looking down at the ground. "Landon said you might have some ideas to help me." She smoothed down her wrinkled shirt and looked up fleetingly, then to the door of the restaurant.

"Let's go eat. We can chat inside," I pasted on a smile and reminded myself that my problems were nothing compared to BeeBee and the challenge she was facing of creating a whole new life.

The smell of chicken was thick enough to cut, and the sound of grease popping in the kitchen conjured up images of crisp golden French fries and perfectly crunchy chicken skin. Yum! We each ordered a chicken wing combo basket with fries and a drink.

Embarrassment tinged BeeBee's cheeks as Sam picked up the tab. She wrung her hands together. "Thank you. I'll pay you back as soon as I can." Her eyes fluttered downward again and my heart squeezed in sympathy for this young girl.

"Why? I'm not paying her back," I smiled as BeeBee looked up at me in shock. "Her parents are loaded, don't worry about it." I winked at BeeBee at patted Sam on the back. My friend rolled her eyes.

"It's my pleasure," Sam told BeeBee, then handed each of us our cups to fill at the drink station.

As we waited for our order number to be called, we settled into a corner booth in a pretty empty section of the small restaurant.

"I don't really know how you can help," BeeBee started. "Landon said you would be good to talk to, and since I met you when you were trying to help him and discover who killed Coco," she gulped. "Well, I thought it was worth a shot because you seemed like nice people and to be honest, I haven't had a whole lot of nice people in my life."

I nodded.

Sam reached out and covered BeeBee's hand, giving it an encouraging squeeze.

Continuing, BeeBee said, "I know I need to get a job, but not many people are going to hire me. Landon said you own a bakery. I can clean floors, ovens, windows, you name it."

I glanced beside me at Sam. Her disappointed look told me my assumption was right; our finances couldn't take the addition of one more employee right now.

"I wish that we could," Sam began.

BeeBee's eyes shuttered, and then her face went blank. I shuddered to think how many times the girl had worn that look, careful not to reveal emotion, not to get invested in anything or anyone.

"How old are you BeeBee?" Curiosity outweighed tact and I asked the question that had been in my mind since we met BeeBee at the massage parlor on our search for answers about the murders at The Cove's Cabins last weekend.

"Seventeen," she jutted her chin out in defense.

I simply nodded as my gut clenched. Seventeen. I tamped down the many other questions threatening to spill out of me: where were her parents; how did she end up at that massage parlor; how long had she been there; what had she suffered?

"But I think I know someone else who could use some extra help." Sam continued.

"Flo?" I asked her. At her nod, I turned back to BeeBee. "That's right, our friend Flo runs the flower shop in Seashell Bay. It is literally right next door to our bakery."

Sam picked up the description. "It's beautiful. Flowers everywhere, vibrant colors, the whole store so full of life."

"And you're sure she needs help?"

I grinned, catching BeeBee's eyes. "Absolutely. She's been borrowing one of our employees on a temporary basis. You would be just the person to get her out of a bind. Her business has picked up with a sale we are running and Flo is worried about getting behind on orders."

"I'll text her right now and see what she says," Sam pulled her phone out of her purse. The purse today was covered in giant daisies, matching the tiny ones all over her outfit.

A throat clearing at the end of our booth demanded attention. We were surprised to find a middle-aged woman scowling at us. "Number 27?" She asked. At our nod, she thrust our tray of food onto the table and stomped off.

"Our bad," I mumbled. "I guess we didn't hear the number called." I shrugged and rolled my eyes at Sam and BeeBee, surprised at the woman's attitude. "Oh well, dig in."

Sam's phone chimed halfway through the meal. She read the screen and then laughed out loud before telling us it was from Flo. "She says can you start today?"

BeeBee smiled, but the smile faded. "Is there a shelter somewhere in your town for women like me?" She busied her fingers moving her fries around in the basket.

"I don't know what you mean by women like you," I said. "If you mean women who were taken advantage of, hurt, and trapped, women who survived, escaped, and chose to change their lives, yes, there is probably a shelter for women like that who need a helping hand. However, that isn't where you are going."

"Nope." Sam butted in. "You're coming to stay with one of us. Or both of us for a few days, Piper shouldn't really be staying alone right now anyway."

"I couldn't put you out like that," BeeBee shook her head.

"No arguments. If you want a ride to Seashell Bay, you have to accept the offer." I winked, trying to lessen the demand of my words.

"Thanks," BeeBee nodded before shoving the last of her chicken wings into her mouth.

Ten minutes later, full and feeling like I weighed five extra pounds that were all grease, I climbed into the passenger seat of Sam's car and buckled my seatbelt. BeeBee had folded herself into the narrow backseat behind me.

"Where should we go to pick up your things?" Sam asked as she looked at BeeBee in the rearview mirror.

"Things?" BeeBee's brow crinkled up.

"Yeah, your clothes and shoes, toothbrush, stuff like that."

The young girl slid a hand into her shorts pocket and held up a tube as long as my index finger. Popping the cap off to reveal a travel toothbrush, she shrugged. "I'm all packed."

Sam narrowed her eyes. "Are you telling me you don't have any clothes or belongings you need before you move to a whole new town?"

BeeBee shook her head. "Nothing that was really mine, and nothing the police haven't probably gotten rid of by now."

My breathing stuttered at the thought of being in BeeBee's place. I really hoped with all my heart that we could help this sweet girl; I didn't know where to start, but I knew I would do whatever it took to show her she was important and valued.

Sam frowned further still, and then suddenly lit up like a kid on Christmas, rapidly tapping her fingers on the steering wheel.

"Oh boy," I said. "Brace yourself, BeeBee. I know that look."

"What look?" BeeBee asked as she slipped the toothbrush back in her pocket.

I pointed at Sam. "The look that says Sam just found the perfect excuse for an impromptu shopping spree."

No amount of protests would change her mind, a fact that I already knew and BeeBee soon learned.

"Thank goodness this outlet mall was on the way home," Sam maneuvered the small car into a tight parking spot right near the entrance to a clothing store.

"Yes, thank goodness," I said sarcastically, throwing in an eye-roll for good measure.

BeeBee got out and stretched her legs.

"Kind of cramped back there," Sam admitted. "Sorry about that."

"No worries, I've been in worse." BeeBee walked over to the sidewalk, leaving Sam and me to look at each other and wonder over that remark.

"Now, I really don't need much," BeeBee insisted as she held the door open for Sam and me to enter the store. "I'll buy more after I have a job for a while."

I shook my head. It was useless. This girl was about to get an entirely new wardrobe and Sam would love every minute of it; I knew this from experience the first time I let her take me shopping in college. I think I still had clothes in my closet from that trip that I hadn't worn yet.

"What kind of clothes do you like?" Sam asked. "Dresses, skirts, sporty, casual, colorful, dark?"

BeeBee's eyes bulged.

"Why don't we take it slow," I nudged Sam in the ribs. "She needs some pants and some t-shirts for work. How about we start with those?"

"You're no fun," Sam grouched.

We made our way to the Junior's section of clothing and after a few moments BeeBee was swept up in Sam's excitement; they pulled out several shirts and two pairs of jeans for BeeBee to try on.

"Do you have a favorite color?" Sam asked BeeBee.

"Umm, light purple," BeeBee said from the other side of the dressing room door.

I selected a couple more shirts, in various shades of purple, and added them to the pile.

Each time that BeeBee emerged from the dressing room, her smile had grown bigger than the last. Before long she was laughing and posing as we clapped or booed. We each picked out our favorite shirt on her, and Sam made BeeBee choose three more that she liked to purchase as well. A mixture of pinks, purples, and maroons mostly, one shirt was a hit with all of us. It was a pastel pink color with a swirling cloud of butterflies on the back; the front had one bigger butterfly resting on the corner of the first letter of the words *Just when the caterpillar thought the world was ending, it became a butterfly.*

"Next stop, cute and fun clothes." Sam led the way next door into a more fashionable, upscale boutique.

Sam insisted BeeBee find at least three outfits in this store, and decided that she and I should shop for a new one, too. "Since we're already here," she reasoned.

While we wondered to and from the racks and the dressing room, BeeBee asked, "Why is it Sam said you don't need to stay alone right now?"

"Some people connected to Asnee have been after me," I explained the happenings of the last few days. "You don't happen to know what that guy's name might be, do you?" I asked at the end as we went into separate stalls to try on a few more clothes.

BeeBee did not know, and I stifled a sigh of disappointment. Bummer. It would have been great if she did, or better yet if she had an address that we could turn over to the police. Then again, I was also relieved. The last thing I wanted was for her to be dragged into any more of this mess; she had lived with it clouding her life for long enough.

"It's perfect!" Sam's elated squeal came from a door or two over. "Piper, BeeBee, what do you think?"

I peeked my head out of my own stall. A door opened on the end and Sam twirled her way over, stopping in front of me. She wore a red and white striped dress with a fitted bodice and wide skirt that stopped right above her knees. The back, I saw when she spun, had a large triangular cutout.

"For the Independence Day Parade," she told us.

"You look beautiful." It was the truth, though she always did. "The dress is fun and casual and you'll stay cool if the weather is as hot as it promises to be," I nodded, affirming her decision. That's what shopping with friends is for, after all.

"What did you two find?" she asked.

BeeBee came out of the room next to me. She wore a floor-length navy maxi dress with shooting stars across the skirt.

Sam clapped. "Gorgeous," she pulled BeeBee to her side and clicked a few selfies.

"Your turn," Sam crooked a finger at me and beckoned.

"I'm not sure," I showed the girls the two outfits I couldn't choose between.

Sam waved a hand. "Get them both," she said. "The square-necked blouse and capris will be perfect for the parade. The sundress, on the other hand, you can wear tonight for the news interview and your date with Griff."

I looked back at the mirror, at the tie-dye blue and white dress that I wore; it had short sleeves which would cover my stitches. The bottom was a hi-low cut and the top was a conservative round neck.

"Okay," I agreed.

After a quick stop for shoes, only BeeBee this time, Sam called it quits on the shopping.

"Wow! That was a lot of shopping," BeeBee murmured to me. "I think I might be dizzy from all the dressing rooms."

"You should count yourself lucky that we were on a time crunch today. We spent less than two hours at the mall. Sam could do this for an entire weekend straight."

BeeBee's jaw dropped. I nodded that it was true and slid into the car laughing.

Nearly another hour later, BeeBee was fast asleep, sprawled across the backseat. I had a book pulled up on my phone, reading to pass the time when Sam reached over and tapped my arm.

"Huh?"

"I think that car back there is following us," Sam lifted her eyes to the rearview mirror, keeping her voice low.

I checked the side view mirror on my side of the car. I could barely make out a dark-colored vehicle about two car lengths behind us. "What makes you think that?" I whispered. "They seem pretty far back to me."

"That's why it is odd. I've been going ten miles per hour under the speed limit for about half an hour. Everyone and their dog has passed me, but not that car; they just hang tight." She pressed the gas pedal. "Watch this."

Sure enough, the car behind us sped up as well, maintaining enough distance that I couldn't read the license plate numbers, but staying close enough that if Sam turned off the windy coastal road, they would know.

"Slow back down," I suggested, "but this time go way under the speed limit. Surely then they will have no choice but to pass us."

Sam nodded and backed off the gas pedal again, letting the car slow naturally as we coasted up a small hill, rather than tapping the breaks. For a moment, it seemed the plan hadn't worked. The dark car behind us slowed to a crawl.

"Oh good!" Sam said as the car sped up and gained on us. "It looks like they are going to pass us after all."

I watched in my mirror. "And they aren't the only ones," I noted as the dark car pulled into the oncoming lane to go around us. "Must have been blocking traffic behind them because this guy is speeding." A second car was closing in fast to our bumper.

Crunch!

Before we realized what was happening, the dark car swerved into the driver's side of Sam's Juke again. Crash!

BeeBee screamed, jerked awake, but thankfully still buckled in.

I watched in horror as Sam's head banged against the window and her hands slipped from the wheel. The black car sped away as I flailed desperately to grab the wheel and keep us on the shoulder of the road rather than careening into the ditch. Thank God - Sam's foot must have come off of the gas pedal as well, or the car died, because after what felt like the most terrifying years of my life, and which equated probably a single hot minute, the car coasted to a stop. I didn't care why or how; I was simply grateful.

"BeeBee," I yelled frantically. "Call 911. I have to get Sam." I scrambled to unbuckle my seatbelt but my shaking hands weren't cooperating. As I leaned over the buckle, pleading with it to let go, I noticed movement. The car behind us had pulled over. *Thank goodness! They must have witnessed the accident.*

As my buckle finally released, I breathed a sigh of relief. It would be fine. I got on my knees and worked to unbuckle Sam's seatbelt. She remained slumped against the door.

I could hear BeeBee talking to dispatch on her cell phone.

"Piper, where are we?" she asked through tears.

Shoot, she was sleeping and has no clue where we are at. I rattled off the last road signs I had noticed to BeeBee and continued to peal the seatbelt away from Sam. Odd that the airbags hadn't gone off, but maybe for the best as I wouldn't have been able to reach her as easily.

The slam of a car door pulled my attention from Sam for a second. I looked through the back glass and fear rippled through me. Our good Samaritan wasn't so good, after all.

Chapter 15

"They're sending an ambulance," BeeBee said.

"BeeBee," I looked to the frightened girl. "Are you hurt?"

She shook her head while looking down at her arms and legs. "No, I don't think so."

"Good," I told her. "Now listen and don't talk." She nodded and I continued. "I need you to duck down low, fold down that seat and crawl into the trunk. Now," I demanded when she seemed about to argue.

"That man we told you about, he's coming up to the car. Get out of sight, now." I whispered harshly.

"Sam," I tried to gently shake my friend. The only thing keeping me remotely sane at the moment was that I could see her chest rising and falling, her breathing steady. That was good. Now I just had to keep it that way.

I watched as BeeBee closed herself into the trunk as instructed.

I warred with myself between the need to see where the tattooed man was now and pretending to be oblivious to his presence and buy more time; I thought that he was the type to want to gloat and be sure I knew he won, so I opted to keep my head down and actions focused on Sam. Her eyelids fluttered open, then closed again. I choked back a sob.

"Please, please, please," I uttered my desperate prayer over and over, no words could contain my emotion, no eloquence convey my need. God knew, and I prayed with all my heart.

I chanced a peek and caught sight of the man stealing up behind the car, almost to the back door. My stomach dropped. Before I could decide what to do, the most beautiful sound reached my ears: sirens!

Real sirens. Not the panic button, not a ringtone; actual sirens attached to an official vehicle of some sort blared.

The man bolted to his running car and pulled a U-turn, tires screaming, as a lone State Trooper screeched to a stop next to our wrecked vehicle. I could hear the officer relaying information over his radio even as he approached the ditch and my side of the car.

I fought as he tried to pull me out; I tried to make him understand that I needed to get Sam. At last his voice, his rational instructions, his demand that I do not do anything to make her worse broke through the panicked fog of my brain. I allowed him to help me out of the vehicle so that he could see to Sam but refused to sit down. I let the backseat down and helped BeeBee out of the car, hugging her close as we cried silent tears.

If the officer were surprised, he didn't show it. Instead, he continued the ministrations he was doing for Sam. He had brought a small emergency kit and first carefully bandaged her head where there was a small gash. I heard him saying there wasn't a lot of bleeding and tuned back into the conversation.

"The ambulance is less than two minutes out," he told me. "I was four minutes away when the call came over dispatch. You're lucky, this is a long stretch of road between towns."

I nodded. He didn't know the half of it.

"My phone, can I get my phone?" I asked minutes later as two EMT's rolled Sam into the back of the ambulance on a stretcher. She had woken briefly two more times but was unable to stay awake. I needed to call Griff. He had to know, had to meet us at the hospital.

The trooper, I hadn't yet managed to retain his name in the chaos of my brain, obliged. He pulled the phone from the floorboard and handed it over. BeeBee and I climbed into the ambulance with Sam and the paramedics.

The trooper had, kindly, offered to take us in his car. I had, not so kindly, informed him he could arrest me or shoot me, maybe both, but otherwise, I wasn't leaving her side. BeeBee latched onto my arm and nodded, so the officer spoke to the paramedics and soon we were on the road.

~

By the time we arrived at the hospital in Seashell Bay, which we had been about forty-five minutes away by car and twenty-five minutes by ambulance, I was crying again. Happy tears this time. Sam had regained consciousness soon after the ambulance doors shut. She remained disoriented and the paramedic warned me not to bother her, so I simply sat, content to hold her hand on one side, BeeBee's on the other.

When the ambulance doors opened and I spotted Griff walking toward us, strong, resolute, and confident, it was everything I needed. He reached for me and I fell right into his arms, my knees giving out. "She woke up," I clung to him. "She woke up, Griff."

Holding me tight, Griff smoothed strands of sweaty, tear-soaked hair out of my face. "And she will be fine," he said.

I nodded, soothed by his calm. I took a deep breath. Pine and leather scents filled my nostrils and I basked in the smell of him. I inhaled again, erasing from my nose and mind the scent of metal, hot roads, dirt, and antiseptic. My head cleared and I dried my eyes with the backs of my hands. *Griff's right. Sam will be okay.*

All three of us, Sam, BeeBee, and I, were admitted to the hospital right away. Griff appeared torn, but I had calmed. The adrenaline had coursed its way through my system, leaving me tired, but capable of taking care of myself. "Go," I told him. "Go with Sam. I'll find you both in a minute."

He gave a slight head shake and the merest hint of a smile. "You better," he joked. The determined expression resumed, mouth set and eyes narrowed. He squeezed my hand and took off after the stretcher, long strides bringing him up beside it in no time where he began to quiz the staff rolling her down the hall.

The nurse allowed BeeBee and I to wait together in a curtained off "room" – I guess walls were getting too expensive – and a doctor came in a scant ten minutes later. I had a seatbelt burn across my chest and some bruising on my elbow. BeeBee sported a large bruise across her stomach since she had been laying down with only the lap belt on.

After much poking and prodding, and insistence from the two of us that we were fine, the doctor released us with a warning to stock up on some over the counter pain meds. "The soreness tomorrow may surprise you," he told us. "Drink lots of water and take something for the inflammation."

We dressed quickly back into our clothes and tossed the hospital gowns into a corner. Swinging the curtain open, I tried to orient myself. *Which way to the front desk?*

"Lowe," a voice screeched. "Not 'low', Lowe – L – O – W – E. It isn't that hard."

My mood deflated faster than a balloon with a hole in it. Deidra. Throwing a fit because someone spelled her last name wrong even though it was an understandable mistake since the words sounded exactly alike.

I motioned BeeBee to follow me and allowed myself to be guided by the sound of general disbelief at the incompetence of *regular* people. "Is there not someone here whose job is to escort me to my daughter? Do you expect me to wander around this place and hope that I make it to her room in time to see her before something terrible happens?" a sharp rap sounded as she slapped the countertop.

That woman was a menace, had never worked a day in her life, and probably couldn't read a hospital floor chart unless it was clearly marked with a trail of diamonds. I watched as the poor unfortunate soul in scrubs nearest her was wrangled into service.

"Mitch, please escort Mrs. LOWE," the nurse at the desk emphasized the name slowly, "to room number 118 in ICU."

"Who is that?" BeeBee asked as I stalked quietly behind them.

"Sam's dear mother," I answered.

"Yikes."

"Exactly." I nodded. "If Sam didn't have a headache before, she will now."

Sam did, of course, already have a headache. Deidra pushed Griff aside, completely ignoring the nurse who had brought her to the room and rushed to Sam as if she might never see her again. It would have been touching if that woman had ever been sincere in her affections for her children in her life.

I swallowed my disgust and slipped in to whisper to Griff. "So?"

"So." He rubbed the back of his neck in that way he does when he's worried or frustrated. "So far, she's got a few spots in her vision and a killer headache. Until a little more of the swelling goes down, the doctor says that Sam has to stay in the hospital."

My hand went to my throat as my heart ached for my friend. Guilt gnawed at me. If I hadn't been with her, this never would have happened. Wait a minute!

"Griff, how did they find me? Us? In the middle of the highway, between towns? In Sam's car, not my truck?" I shook my head. It was too much. "I have to go. I have to get ahold of Sheriff Kent. I'm going to that impound lot to look at that car."

Chapter 16

At five, Sheriff Kent picked BeeBee and me up at the hospital. He wasn't too pleased about it, but then he hadn't been pleased when I told him a taxi could get me to the impound lot all by myself just as easily. He decided to take me himself and make sure trouble didn't find me again. BeeBee came along because we both thought that being with the sheriff should keep us pretty safe. Or safer. At least, I hoped so.

The black gate, sprinkled liberally with rust, swung to the inside with a series of clinks and groans as if the wheels were tired of supported the long metal and wire structure. Inch by slow-moving inch, Sheriff Kent drove the car in following the progress of the gate.

Cars were lined up in long rows, side by side. Old cars, new cars, cars that were barely recognizable beyond being a heap of metal; a few of the latter made me cringe, unsure how anyone could have survived.

"You said it was brought in today, and you're sure it was brought here?" The sheriff asked, and I forced my thoughts back to why we were here.

"Yes, sir. Griff made the phone call to the tow truck driver himself. It is a yellow Nissan Juke and they said it would be delivered here within the hour."

"How long ago was that?"

I pulled my phone out of my pocket to check the time. "A-About an hour," I said sheepishly.

Two gray eyebrows raised over dark sunglasses.

I shrugged.

Just then, the gate started serenading us with the creaking, groaning ruckus again. I swiveled my head in the seat. "Look, that's it now." I smiled at the sheriff. He pointedly ignored me and pulled the car to the side, out of the way of the tow truck.

We stepped out of the vehicle and, while the sheriff spoke to the driver, BeeBee and I waited to the side. I tapped my foot on the ground, impatient to confirm my suspicions. At last, the car had been unloaded and was settled into a space at the end of the row nearest the gate.

I hurried over and knelt on the ground, craning my neck to see under the car. After frustrating seconds spent in the dirt, I sat back on my heels.

The sheriff stood watching me, arms crossed. He jerked a thumb over his shoulder and I moved out of his way as directed.

Sheriff Kent pulled an electronic wand from a bag by his feet, a bag I hadn't noticed him retrieve in my rush to prove a point, and methodically worked his way around the undercarriage of the car. Soon enough, a beep sounded and an orange light began blinking on the wand.

I knew it!

"Same type of device we found on your truck, Miss Rivers." Sheriff Kent bagged the small black object.

"May I?" I asked, holding out my hand for the bag. The sheriff hesitated. "I won't touch it or steal it, Sheriff. I'd like to look at it more closely though. Who knows, when I might need to be able to recognize one of these things as often as they keep showing up?"

With a curt nod, Sheriff Kent handed me the sealed bag and left me to examine it as he put away his tools. He agreed that we could get our shopping bags and any other personal belongings out of the beat-up car. Sam would be heartbroken when she found out.

"This little thing is what let them almost kill us today?" BeeBee shuddered.

"Yes. It seems like they are a very determined group. I just wish I could figure out where they are; obviously, they're sticking close. It would have made more sense for them to move on to somewhere new when their operation was discovered."

BeeBee's brow furrowed. "It seems like Asnee was part of some brotherhood. Maybe revenge is more important to this man who's after you than escape?"

I pondered that but had no time to continue the discussion before the sheriff approached. "You ladies ready to go? I'll have a deputy come do a full work-up of the car, look for prints or evidence." He took his sunglasses off then and looked at me. "I wouldn't get your hopes up for much since your truck turned up clean. I'm going to assign a unit to patrol that bakery where you work more often, but, Miss Rivers, I can't advise you enough to be careful and pay attention." He spun his gaze to BeeBee, including her in the warning. "Both of you. This guy has gotten very close to getting rid of you, not once but twice. Let's not let him have a chance for the third time to be the charm, understood?"

I gulped. For a man of few words, the sheriff sure packed a punch when he did speak. "Understood." I gave a wooden nod.

Satisfied, he put his shades back on and we headed to the car. A somber ride took us back to the hospital. I knew the sheriff was right, still, it ate at me that there was nothing I was supposed to do but sit around and hope not to be killed. We needed more information, some kind of a break in the case of the scary tattooed man. I had a bad feeling that we wouldn't find him until he found me again.

Before I opened the door, I decided to ask for another favor. "Sheriff, do you have a man you can spare or someone you can call in to post watch over my friend Sam in the hospital here?" I wiped at a rogue tear. "She may have to stay awhile and I don't want someone hurting her more to get to me."

"I'll get it done," he promised.

I smiled and hoped he knew how much I meant it when I said, "Thank you. For everything."

BeeBee and I exited the car and made our way back through the lobby and toward the back hallway where Sam's room was. The scene before me when we arrived wasn't what I expected to find.

Chapter 17

I blinked a few times to make sure I wasn't the one suffering from a head injury. Nope. The scene didn't change.

The curtains were drawn shut, and a lamp in the corner was turned on but no other lights. Sam's bed was raised to a sitting position, but she had her head tilted back, face toward the ceiling. Her hands covered her eyes. Two chairs were pulled near her bed, Griff was nowhere to be seen, but Landon appeared to have hemmed Deidra into the far chair in the corner and a heated debate could be heard.

"Landon?" At my voice, he turned. Sam uncovered her eyes, lips stretching into a smile.

"Lovely, you're here," Deidra's sneer belied the tight-lipped fake smile and positivity she pretended to convey.

Rather than unfurl my own insults, specifically my surprise at her ability to pry herself away from the many pressing activities someone as important as she always had, I bit my tongue. Ignoring Deidra completely, instead, I asked, "Landon, what are you doing here?"

"I came as soon as BeeBee texted me," he said.

That explained it. I felt a little bad that I hadn't thought to text him, but it had been a crazy afternoon. I mouthed *thanks* to BeeBee who nodded. She hovered at the edge of the door, looking unsure of herself.

"Where's Griff?" I asked, turning back to the group. "Sam, how are you feeling?" I approached the other side of her hospital bed and took her hand.

"Better," she said. "And my brother went to get Mother her special coffee."

"What kind of hospital won't even make a decent Frappuccino as part of the room service menu?" Deidra snapped.

The kind who isn't here to serve you but to save people like your daughter who are injured or sick. Boy, when Sam got out of here, I planned to request a medal for keeping all of these thoughts to myself. Or at least a gold star. Maybe a golden cookie. I focused my attention back on Sam. "The headache?" I raised my eyebrows, daring her to lie to me.

"Still hurts like the devil," she admitted. "But the spots in my vision cleared up and the doctors were really pleased about that."

"Good." I squeezed her hand.

"The scan came back," Landon chimed in. "While I was here," he explained. "They said miraculously there was no skull fracture sustained."

"BeeBee," Sam called softly. "Come on in. How about you two?" she moved her head slowly between us, careful not to make fast motions. "Were you both alright?"

I nodded and let BeeBee answer as she came to stand next to me. "Minor bruising. We're good, don't worry."

"I'm glad to hear that," Sam smiled again.

"Looks like I'm missing the party," Griff ambled into the room with a Grande Frappuccino from the major coffee chain around the corner. "Here you go, Mother." He handed it across the bed to Deidra. She didn't utter a word of thanks, not that that was surprising; she probably would have preferred a large bottle of wine.

"That's better," Deidra said as she sipped the steaming liquid. She rose, "Well, I'd love to stay but it is getting a bit crowded and I have several appointments to get to before the spa closes. You understand I'm sure? This has all been so stressful for me." she patted Sam on the shoulder. "If you get out of here by tomorrow, call Rosalind and have her set up a lunch."

Deidra eyed Landon until he stood and scooted his chair out of her way, then she sauntered out of the room. I could hear her talking faintly down the hallway, as she called and ordered her driver to be ready to leave.

"Wow." BeeBee stared after the departing figure.

"Yep. Told you she was a real character," I said. "Landon, what were you two so worked up about when I got here?"

Sam chuckled and then winced and rubbed her head. The smile dimmed as her face sagged with exhaustion.

"Equality of the social classes based on their humanity, not their net worth."

I raised my eyebrows at Landon's answer. "I'm not even going to ask how that was going," I turned to Griff. "No wonder you went to get the coffee. I thought that was a bit odd for you to go to such lengths for one of Deidra's demands. It's all making sense now," I laughed.

"Yeah and none of them cared that I couldn't escape and was subjected to the whole ludicrous argument," Sam stared up at the ceiling again.

"Had to see if she was as bad as she sounded," Landon defended himself.

"And?" I prompted.

"And she's worse," he conceded. "Especially the way she treats Sam," he scowled and his voice grew heavy with emotion.

Considering the mistreatment that I was certain Landon had witnessed in various places over the years, that statement spoke volumes.

I noticed Sam's eyes drifting shut. She was struggling to stay awake and we were the reason. "Hey Sam," I whispered.

"Hmm?" she turned toward my voice.

"I think we are going to go and let you rest," I told her.

Her eyes opened again and found mine. "You have something important to do," she murmured. "Don't forget."

"Don't forget what?" I asked.

"I don't remember," her lids slipped closed.

My panicked expression must have shown because Griff slipped his hand in mine and led me away from the bed. "The doctors said drowsiness and confusion are normal. They are monitoring her very closely but strongly believe she is out of any true danger."

I swallowed reflexively, trying to bring moisture to my dry mouth. "Okay." From the corner of my eye, I saw a uniformed woman stop at the nurse's station and then make her way to the room we stood in. I greeted her at the door, stepping into the hallway to speak quietly. Griff followed.

After I assured myself the deputy had all of the knowledge that I could give her, including a description of the tattooed man and how dangerous he was, Griff and I went back into the room.

"I'm going to stay a little longer," Griff told me. "You're welcome to stay, or I can come to pick you up for our dinner date later on."

"That's what Sam was telling me not to forget!" I looked at my phone. There was still time. "I have to be at the bakery soon, to give a quick statement about the Fourth of July sale that Flo's Flowers and the Ooey Gooey Bakery is putting on. Sam set it up and somehow failed to tell me about it until this afternoon."

"I can give you a ride," Landon offered. "You too, BeeBee. Didn't your text say that you would be working at the flower shop?"

BeeBee nodded. "That's right. Thanks, Landon."

"That would be great," I agreed. "Griff, I'll see you later. If Sam wakes, please give her my love."

Chapter 18

"We've got about twenty minutes to get to the bakery before Missy will be there with the news van." I climbed into Landon's car.

BeeBee placed all of the shopping bags in the backseat before scooting in beside them. "That should give me a few minutes to change clothes and introduce you to Flo," I turned to look at her as I buckled my seatbelt.

"Don't worry, we'll be there in a flash," Landon assured me.

I breathed out and rehearsed what I would say in my head. He was right, we would be there and soon it would be over.

So much for the power of positive thinking.

Landon was wrong.

Two blocks from the bakery, traffic was at a complete halt. "What is going on?" I leaned forward in my seat, trying to see any reason for the delay.

"Over there," Landon pointed just ahead to the left. Plumes of smoke sliced through the clear sky; flames licked the top of an electrical pole and the tops of the trees nearest to it. Two fire engines had set up a perimeter, and it looked like trucks from the electric company were being routed in between cars as well.

"You have got to be kidding me," I shook my head. "There's been no storm, no lightning. What, did the transformer thing explode or spontaneously combust?" We sat there watching as firemen continued to evacuate nearby buildings, and otherwise maintained a perimeter. As the vehicles bearing the electric company logo arrived, a single individual in a white hat approached one of the firemen. They seemed to be making some kind of plan, hands motioned and heads nodded frequently.

Landon fiddled with buttons on the radio until a local newscast came on, then turned the volume up more. As it turned out, yes, the transformer did explode. No confirmation was available for the exact why it happened, according to the news report, but suggestions of old wiring or power surge were being tossed around.

"Now what?" I slumped back in the seat.

"Why aren't they putting it out?" BeeBee asked, pointing to the firefighters who still worked to maintain a large perimeter and ushered bystanders back.

"They're probably waiting for the electric company to confirm all power to this spot has been shut off," Landon remarked. At our puzzled faces, he explained further. "If those wires fall," he pointed to the four wires attached to the fiery pole top, "then they could spark and cause more structure fires or kill someone if they are still full of electricity."

Before I had time to marvel at the constantly surprising depths of knowledge my friend had, a flurry of activity distracted me. Sure enough, Mr. White Hat spoke into a radio and then spoke again to the fireman standing by. Soon hoses were spraying water at the trees and a large expanding white foam, like the kind in fire extinguishers I assumed, onto the pole.

BeeBee, in the meantime, had evidently been looking up things on her phone because she leaned forward and held it up for Landon and me to see. "Look, Landon is right. This article says that spraying water on a pole fire, or any electrical fire actually, can allow the electricity to travel through the hose stream of water and often result in electrocution."

"I guess that makes sense," I nodded as I considered this new information. "I mean, everyone knows not to turn on the power to an appliance at home if the appliance is in water or really wet. Like the movies when someone is killed in the bathtub by tossing in a small, plugged-in toaster."

Landon cocked his head to the side.

"I'm just saying." I shrugged. "Oh! We're finally moving." The line of cars rolled slowly forward as a woman in a bright neon vest routed traffic down a side road.

"I'm not sure how to get to the bakery from here," Landon said as we took the detour.

I waved him forward. "You go straight a block and take a left. We can come up behind the bakery faster this way anyway." A glance at my phone showed that we might just make it. And when I say just, I mean by the skin of my teeth, the hair on my chinny-chin-chin, and all those other bewildering expressions.

Landon pulled into the rear parking lot eight minutes later. Not that I was counting, or slavishly watching the minutes tick by on my phone. Nope. Not at all.

I rushed to the back door and turned the handle. Locked.

I wasted another half a minute fishing my keys out of my pocket. At last, I made it inside, not waiting for Landon or BeeBee, simply whooshing past Victoria, and making a beeline for the swinging door.

I didn't have my pretty new dress. I didn't even have a hairbrush. I did have a new determination, however; a determination to conquer the public speaking fear, a determination to help Flo's business, a determination to do this and make Sam proud. I had managed to talk to Missy on camera once before when we won the fundraising contest. I could manage it again.

I decided right then that, if practice makes perfect, I would speak to a crowd of people many times over if it meant when I sat down in court Monday, the words would flow easily and clearly enough from my testimony to leave no doubt about the guilt of Regina and Asnee.

"Piper! There you are," Gladys stopped wiping the counter and bustled over to me as I entered the café from the kitchen. "There's some hoity-toity news lady over in the corner and she's not very happy. Wouldn't even accept a complimentary dessert while she waited." Gladys harrumphed. "I didn't know what to tell her except that I was certain you or Sam would be here soon."

That stopped me in my tracks. "Gladys, I'm so sorry. There was absolutely no time to tell you.

It's been such a nightmare of an afternoon." I caught my breath. I wasn't on camera yet and here I was, already about to hyperventilate. "Sam is in the hospital. She's going to be okay, but there was a car accident."

Gladys's mouth went slack and she began wringing the dish towel in her hand.

Taking Gladys by the arms, I promised to tell her everything in a minute. "As soon as I'm done; I have to take care of this first," I said gesturing to Missy. "It's something Sam asked me to do."

I walked to the corner to face the news diva, racking my brain for her last name as I went. She sat with her back rigid, her legs crossed and her long hot-pink manicured fingernails clicking away on the top of the table so hard I feared she would wreck Millie's paint job. Her camera boy, a different youth than the last time, sat a table away from her and he appeared to be happily munching on an Oatmeal Chocolate No-Bake Cookie.

"Miss Sims," I spoke first, relieved the name had come forward at last. "I'm so sorry to have kept you waiting. I'm ready to start as soon as you are."

"Really?" she looked down her nose at my wrinkled shirt, cargo pants, and sneakers. "You wouldn't like a moment to...ahum...freshen up?" She made no move to stand. I darted my eyes to the camera boy who inclined his head, eyes wide, as if telling me to hurry and go now.

I smiled broadly to show that I was perfectly comfortable with my appearance. "Not at all. Please, I'm quite ready and I'm certain you are a busy woman with things to do, as am I." I wouldn't be intimidated by the likes of miss-prissy, not when I'd been nearly murdered twice in as many days. "Would you prefer to set up inside or outside?" I asked, the sugary sweetness of my own voice tasting sour in my mouth.

"Inside. The heat out there is dreadful," Missy stretched her long legs and got to her feet. Immediately, the camera boy jumped to attention.

As I ran my tongue around my dry mouth, I wished I had been a little less stubborn; maybe grabbed a drink and one of the advertisement flyers when Missy had offered me extra time. Too late now.

Once the camera and I were positioned exactly as Missy dictated, her pinched and annoyed expression transformed into one of charm and happiness. She nodded at the camera boy. A red light flared to life on the camera and we were rolling.

"Good evening, Seashell Bay!" Missy glowed, reveling in the spotlight. "I'm here this evening with Ooey Gooey Bakery proprietor Piper

Rivers. Piper," her head swiveled to me for two seconds and then back to the camera. "It's my understanding you want to share some exciting news with the residents of Seashell Bay?"

As she was speaking, I noticed Flo had walked in and stood behind the camera boy. Flo held up one of the mixed bouquets and I smiled. Thank goodness.

I took a deep breath and launched into the announcement I had been practicing repeatedly in my head when we were setting up to film.

"Good evening, Missy. Thank you for being here." I turned to the camera, my palms sweating and my heart rate thumping out a whole new rhythm. A few customers now stood and watched as well, having trickled in behind Flo. I thought of the courtroom full of people. I thought of Flo's business and of Sam in the hospital. I planted my feet a little wider apart and waved. *Here goes nothing.* "Hi, friends, neighbors. Thank you for watching as well. I am excited to have this chance to tell you about our biggest sale this season which also happens to be a cross-promotional sale with Flo's Flowers." I reeled off a few facts about the sale and the coupons and then described the mixed flower-cookie bouquets. "Here to demonstrate one for you is Flo herself. Flo, would you join me?" I asked, ignoring the slip of Missy's smile as I brought Flo in front of the camera and crowded Missy a bit out of the center frame.

Flo held the bouquet up in front of her face, making me relax the last little bit as I stifled a laugh. I might not be the only publicity shy person around. Gently, I pushed the bouquet down a few inches while pointing to and describing a few of the cookies: Party Sparklers, a treat filled with PopRocks for a fun sizzle and fizz; Strawberry Shortbread; Blueberry Shortbread; Fun-Loving Flag Cookies, a simple sugar cookie decorated with frosting to look like the country's flag.

"Flo, would you tell us about some of these flowers. I notice this bouquet has way more than a bunch of flowers dyed artificial colors."

Flo took a faltering step backward. I recognized that deer in headlights look and drew her attention to a specific flower. "Tell me about these delicate little blue ones."

Her eyes followed my finger. "Oh! Those are Forget-Me-Nots." Flo smiled up at me. "I thought they were more than appropriate for an Independence Day centerpiece when we are celebrating the day the Declaration of Independence was adopted in 1776. That is a long way back to remember, after all."

"That is so true, and how thoughtful that you chose those flowers for that specific reason. Do all flowers have meaning?" I asked, genuinely curious now.

"Well, yes, traditionally speaking there is meaning behind most flowers though some aren't well-known or acknowledged. I enjoy learning about them and incorporating the absolutely perfect flowers into the orders that people bring in, whether they want to convey love, thankfulness, well-wishes, or maybe just friendship," Flo added slyly. We shared a laugh over that, remembering her surprise at my request for breakup flowers.

Having shared her space long enough, Missy stepped in front of us to close out the segment. In seconds, the camera light was off and Missy was snapping commands like an army general at the camera boy. I hurried to the counter and came back as they were leaving, managing to sneak the poor kid a to-go bag while he held the door open for Missy to exit.

"Thank you," he said.

"You looked like you could use a few more," I smiled.

"I don't know what I could use, but these will definitely help."

I turned away from the door and saw Gladys waiting for me at the counter. Flo waved and headed back to the flower shop, with several potential customers tagging along beside her and asking questions.

"Flo wanted to leave this here for a display," Gladys scooted the mixed bouquet over to me.

"Perfect!" I scooted it to the center of the display case where it would be sure to draw attention. "Do we have anymore…" I smiled my thanks as Gladys pulled a stack of flyers from under the register before my sentence was finished. Scattering them around the bouquet, I stepped back to survey my work. "There we go," I said.

"Why is Sam in the hospital?" Gladys asked.

"Let's close up early and I'll tell you everything." Closing at eight instead of nine couldn't hurt and I for one wasn't up for a bout of customer service right now anyway. I felt like I had lived three days squeezed into one, so much had happened.

~

In the kitchen, we found Victoria putting BeeBee to work as a taste-tester. "Gladys, this is BeeBee. BeeBee, my friend Gladys."

When I asked about Landon, BeeBee told me that he had left after making sure she was comfortable with Victoria. With introductions out of the way, I gave Gladys and Victoria the general rundown of our afternoon.

"I'm going up there right now to see Sam," Gladys untied her apron strings. "Do you want to ride with me?"

I shook my head. "Griff is picking me up for dinner."

"Good." With a firm nod, Gladys grabbed her purse from a hook on the wall. "You two deserve a bit of a rest. You've been through more than enough these past few weeks."

I couldn't agree more. I hugged her, and with a tip to take a different route in case there was still clean-up going on from the fire, unlocked the front door for her to leave. Relocking the door, I surveyed the café. There wasn't too much that needed to be done in the way of cleanup. Just a quick sweep would take care of it.

Victoria must have read my mind. "Piper," she said as I returned to the kitchen. "Do you want me to clean up while you take BeeBee next door to meet Flo?"

"Do you mind?" I asked.

"No, I'm waiting on Millie to finish up anyway. We're going to get burgers and milkshakes for a late treat; we skipped supper." Victoria turned to BeeBee. "You should come, too. Unless you have plans?"

Oh gosh – I'm such a horrible person that I hadn't even considered what to do with BeeBee while Griff and I were on our date. Of course, I wouldn't simply abandon her; besides, Griff would understand if she needed to come. Still.... "If you want to go with Victoria and Millie, then I can meet y'all after and pick you up," I told her. "We've had a long day though and if you want a raincheck, I'm sure the girls would understand."

"We definitely would," Victoria nodded. "You two go to Flo's and BeeBee you can decide before we all leave."

BeeBee smiled. "Okay."

We used the back door and walked the few feet over to the back side of Flo's Flowers. I knocked on the door. With everything going on lately, we had both gotten into better habits of keeping things locked up tight.

Flo answered and welcomed us inside. The fragrances floating in the room were so different from that of the bakery. Both were incredible and sweet, but unique; the bakery smelled delicious while Flo's Flowers could be described more as invigorating. The Ooey Gooey Bakery could make your mouth water and your stomach growl; Flo's Flowers made me want to run barefoot or dance in the rain.

"BeeBee, this is Flo and Millie." I pointed to each in turn. Millie smiled and waved the greenery she was holding.

"Nice to meet you," Flo reached out a hand for BeeBee to shake. "I'm so glad you're here."

"Thank you," BeeBee brushed hair behind her ears. "I don't really know anything about flowers," she told Flo, "but it smells very nice in here."

"It does, doesn't it? Don't worry about what you do or don't know. To be honest, it might be most helpful to me if you started out working the front and taking orders from customers. At least while we're busy. After that, if you want to learn, I can show you some of the things I've been teaching Millie about arranging the flowers themselves."

I stayed to chat with Millie while Flo took BeeBee up front and went over the basics of the cash register, how to run cards, questions to ask when customers filled out the order request, and so on.

When they came back, Flo said it was past time for the flower shop to close as well. We would all be back very early in the morning to get some more work done, though I didn't plan to open the bakery to customers until one tomorrow afternoon. BeeBee and I bid Flo good night and gathered Victoria up from the bakery.

"I think I will go with Victoria and Millie. If you're sure you don't mind?" BeeBee looked to me for an answer.

Griff's truck rumbled into the parking lot right then. "I don't mind at all, but let us give you a ride around front to your scooters. I'm not comfortable with you walking all alone with dusk settling in."

The girls agreed and piled into the backseat of Griff's truck. He simply raised a good-natured eyebrow at me. I bet if I had told him they were all joining us for dinner he wouldn't protest a bit. Tightness squeezed at my chest; I didn't know where I'd gone and had the good dumb luck to attract this wonderful man, but I couldn't be happier about it. Even if he was a bit of a worry-wart and overprotective sometimes. Or all the time.

"Can we drop the girls out front by their scooters, please?" I watched his face.

"Absolutely," he grinned and winked. "Unless they'd rather go to dinner with us?"

192

Chapter 19

"What would you have done if they all said yes?" I asked Griff.

He glanced over at me and back to the road. "Found a cheap place to eat I suppose," he joked.

"Where are we going?" I watched yet another cluster of restaurants blur by the window as we passed without slowing.

"You'll see."

A sneaking suspicion took hold as Griff continued to leave downtown behind. The city traffic disappeared soon as we turned on smaller and smaller roads. Before long, Griff pulled up at a small public beach on the outskirts of a residential neighborhood, far away from the larger areas where summer tourists could be found.

"I thought you might prefer a little peace and quiet to lobster and wine."

"You thought right!" I wiggled my toes, eager to get them out of these shoes and into the sand. "I wasn't too hungry anyway," I said not wanting Griff to feel guilty for not taking me to dinner.

"That's too bad," he said as he stepped out of the truck and walked to the back.

I hopped out of the passenger side and peered closer as he opened the bed of the truck. My eyes widened as he slid out a large red toolbox and a checkered blanket.

"Did you pack a picnic?" I jumped up and down in the sand, clapping. This was too good to be true. Seriously, a kind, decent, honest man AND a romantic? Gladys would just die when I told her.

"Don't worry," Griff walked past me and down the gentle slope of sand toward the water. "You don't have to eat any since you aren't hungry and all. I'm more than capable of taking care of a handful of mozzarella sticks, a few mashed potatoes, snap peas, and freshly-fried salmon patties."

I glared, earning a sharp laugh.

"I will eat the fish, or you will be fed to the fishes," I tried out my best mob impersonation.

"Okay, okay," Griff held up the toolbox. "Here, help me set this up and we can eat before any of it gets cold."

I took the folded blanket and spread it out on a somewhat flat area of sand. I removed my shoes and sat one in each of two corners to help hold it down, before getting comfy on the blanket. One nice thing about summer by the beach, the light of the sun stretched long into the evening.

Griff sat too, placing the toolbox-come-picnic basket on a third corner. From a sliding drawer, he handed me paper plates and real forks. He opened the lid and delicious smells tickled my nose and enticed my tummy. He unpacked multiple containers and then dished all of the food up onto the plates that I held out to him.

"This looks amazing," I told him. "Let's say grace and then dig in."

As I bowed my head, Griff reached over and gripped my hand. There was nothing in the space of those few seconds but the beautiful, rhythmic crashing of waves. "Father in Heaven," he prayed, "thank you for this food and more for someone to share it with. God, thank you for protecting my sister, Piper, and BeeBee today. We pray the madman is caught and we can put all of this behind us. Amen."

I swallowed down the emotion, thick in my throat, and shoved a giant bite of potatoes, the ultimate comfort food, into my mouth. The sunset blazed across the water, turning the ocean into a living mirror, reflecting the gorgeous colors and reaching up to hold more with each swell.

Griff lifted his fork, then put it down on the plate and jogged to the truck. He returned with two bottles of water. "Sorry," he ducked his chin.

"You don't get to apologize when you successfully pulled off the best date a girl could dream of," I shook my finger at him before accepting the bottle of water. The salmon patties were crunchy and full of flavors; I tasted garlic and pepper and could see large crystals of sea salt on the top.

Griff snuck most of the mozzarella sticks onto his plate before I caught on and slapped his hand. "Hey now, I plan to eat my fair share of those, too." He knew I wasn't playing, but he laughed anyway before handing two of them back.

At last, we both cleared our plates. Griff took them and our napkins to the nearest trash can while I stowed the other items back in the toolbox. Even looking at our make-shift picnic basket made me grin. Only Griff. It was so funny and yet so perfect. I spent a little more time than needed placing the empty Tupperware carefully inside, rifling through every drawer in the process.

At last, I struck gold.

Or at least gold wrapping. I palmed the little nuggets and hid them behind me as I slid back to my seat on the blanket before Griff could see.

Sitting down beside me, Griff leaned back on his elbows and we watched the ocean for a few minutes.

"I almost forgot," he said. I looked on as he pulled out the compartment on the toolbox and searched amongst the wrenches in varying sizes. He went through a few more places, coming back to look in the same drawer each time. He turned with narrowed eyes and I whipped my gaze to the sky, trying but failing to tamp down the massive grin on my face.

"Did you eat my dessert?"

"Look how beautiful the stars are," I continued to crane my neck away from him.

"Lady, where is my dessert?" he tried again.

I turned at his stern tone and saw his eyes crinkled in humor. Giving over to the laughter, I pulled the small truffles from underneath my leg and held out one to him. Rather than take it, he grasped my whole hand and brought it to his lips for a kiss.

My breath hitched. The truffle in my other hand would probably be smushed flat, and yes, I am the kind of chocolate-obsessed woman for whom that thought did cross my mind even in this romantic, heart-beating-out-of-my-chest type of moment. Still, truffle or no, I found I couldn't look away from him, as he lowered my hand back down.

I jumped away as my phone beeped, shattering the quiet.

Holy pancakes, cell phones might be the worst invention ever. Or at least the rudest.

Griff stood and carried the toolbox to the truck while I checked my messages. "The girls are done eating; they texted to say they will be in Babbling Books when we are ready to pick BeeBee up." I popped my hazelnut and chocolate truffle into my mouth. Delicious. Then I stood. "I guess we may as well go now; we do both have to be at the bakery and Flo's early in the morning. Plus, I kind of feel like I need to keep an eye on her until the trial is over."

"I'm going to head to the hospital early in the morning to check in on Sam," Griff said as he bent to help me fold up the blanket. I snatched my shoes up and carried them to the truck, shaking the sand out as we went. Griff stepped over and opened my door for me, giving me a hand in. When he removed his hand from mine, he left his truffle, without a word, nestled in my fingers for me to eat. In my book, if you share your dessert with someone, that is a giant gesture. I did a little happy

dance in the seat, not even hesitating before I
popped the candy into my mouth.

Chapter 20

My alarm went off at four o'clock on Sunday morning. I stretched my arms overhead and gave myself a few minutes to fully wake up. I reached for my phone and my hand swung through the air; Sam's nightstand was on the opposite side of the bed than I was used to.

After picking up BeeBee last night from Babbling Books, Griff would only agree to deposit us at my truck if we followed him home and stayed the night in Sam's duplex, where we would have been anyway if she wasn't in the hospital. Too tired to argue, and frankly concerned about putting BeeBee in danger if we went to my apartment, I hadn't taken much convincing.

Finding my phone eventually, I dressed and brushed my teeth quickly. I went down the hall and tapped on the guest room door.

"I'm up," BeeBee's soft voice rang out.

"Tea or coffee?" I asked through the door.

With her answer, I padded to the kitchen to fix our drinks in some portable cups. By the time BeeBee joined me five minutes later, her steaming cup of coffee stood at attention next to the little crowd of creamers and sugar.

"Thanks," she popped the lid on a toasted marshmallow cream and poured a couple of tablespoons into the cup.

"How did you sleep?" I handed her a long, thin spoon to stir the drink.

"Pretty great." Her smile widened. "I think that has to be the softest bed I've ever slept in."

"Good! Now, let's get you over to Flo's Flowers." I grabbed my travel cup full of green tea.

~

By a quarter before eight, Victoria and I had all of the baking done, plus plenty of extra batters made up and chilling in the walk-in fridge.

"That should be plenty to keep you going while I'm at court tomorrow," I told Victoria as I put dishes into the large industrial dishwasher.

"I think I'll go over and see if there is anything I can help out with at Flo's Flowers,"

Victoria said when I told her my plans to go see Sam at the hospital.

"I'll walk you over."

Millie opened the back door for us when I knocked. "Morning!" Her long blonde ponytail bounced with her energetic greeting.

The surprise must have registered on my face when I saw BeeBee working with a lovely bouquet of flowers because Flo began to explain. "BeeBee learned the cash register and front-of-shop business faster than expected this morning."

BeeBee grinned and took over. "Yes, so Flo told me I could practice making an arrangement. What do you think?"

Stepping closer, I admired the bright yellow and deep purple flower combinations that BeeBee had put together. They were not as refined or symmetrical as when Flo finished one of her masterpieces, but they were beautiful and cheerful all the same. They were displayed in a simple white, cylindrical vase. "I think you did great, much better than I would if I were to give it a try."

"Thanks. I planned to give them to Sam at the hospital."

"She will love them!" I turned to Flo. Millie was showing Victoria a few different flowers. "Flo, BeeBee and I are going to the hospital to visit Sam.

I may run a few other errands, and I want to stop by the church and see Pastor Dan before coming to open the Ooey Gooey at one. Text me if you need me to bring you anything."

Flo bobbed her head. "I'll do that, thank you."

In the truck, I sent a text to Griff letting him know that we were on our way. I hesitated with my hand on the keys, not quite bringing myself to crank the truck.

"What's wrong?"

I shook my head. "Probably nothing," I admitted. "But I keep waiting for that psycho to pop up again. I was just thinking about those trackers that keep turning up everywhere. I think I'm going to check the truck before we go."

"I'll help," BeeBee unfastened her seatbelt.

Together, we combed the underneath of my truck the best that we could. My hands were embedded with gravel when I stood. Dusting them off on my pants, I did a last check around the mirrors and under the handle to the tailgate. Nothing out of the ordinary was in any of the places I could think to check, so, giving up, I climbed back in the truck and we headed to the hospital.

When we arrived, I bypassed the front desk and walked straight to Sam's hospital room. "Hey,"

I called out with only a brief tap on the door frame. I came to a stop so fast that BeeBee bumped into. I felt a little water from the vase spill down the small of my back, but that was the least of my concerns.

The man sitting in the chair beside the bed was not Griff.

And, as if that wasn't enough to freak me out on its own, the woman lying in the ICU bed wasn't Sam.

Maybe I had been in too big of a hurry. I was really bad about hurrying. And directions, sometimes I was bad at directions. I likely made a simple mistake. I convinced myself that each of these was a plausible explanation and one of them would be the truth. It was easy to convince yourself of something you wanted to believe.

I stepped back into the hallway and checked the room number.

Nope.

No mistake. A plaque declaring this Room 118 stared back at me. I glanced in the room, looking at the couple who hadn't noticed me because they were wrapped up in each other, hands grasped, tears glistening down the cheek of the woman in the bed.

I didn't need tears. I needed Sam. Or Griff. I spun on my heel and snatched my phone from my pocket all in one motion. BeeBee stumbled back out of my way. I could hear the clapping of her shoes on the waxed floor behind me as I hit call.

Voicemail. Both of their phones went to voicemail.

Plan B. I marched up to the front information desk. "Hi. My friend was here yesterday and now she's gone. At least, someone else is in her room. The thing is, nobody told me she was being discharged so she has to be around here, somewhere, right?" I pasted on my very best I'm-not-a-crazy-person look. "Can you give me any information?"

"Patient name?" The woman asked in a bored voice, never missing a beat as she chomped on her gum and stared at the computer screen.

"Samantha Lowe."

Tapping keys and clicking the mouse, she went through a search engine of some kind. Her clicking slowed at last. All gum chomping ceased as her eyes grew wide. She leaned forward and read words that I couldn't see, no matter how I craned my neck in an attempt to do so.

"Did you find anything?" I asked, unable to take the suspense any longer.

"No."

"What do you mean no?" Worry chewed on my stomach, my brain sent flashes of horrible scenarios around and around in my mind. "You looked her up. You found something. Where is she?" For all the effort, I couldn't keep the anger out of my voice. My calm was unraveling like a ball of yarn on a downhill slope.

"I can't release information on that patient."

"Why not? I came here to see her only yesterday, what in the world changed?" I gripped the countertop and leaned toward the woman. "She's my best friend. You have to tell me something," I begged.

"Miss Lowe is a high-profile individual. She has been remanded into private care and I am not allowed to say that, much less anything else." The woman rolled back in her chair and swiveled to a different computer, away from me.

I resisted the urge to scream or bang on the counters, but barely. It wasn't the nurse's fault; after all, she was only doing her job. I took a deep breath and stepped over to the side where BeeBee waited for me.

"Is Sam okay?" she asked, lip trembling, as she clutched the vase tightly. We may not have known her long, but it seemed we'd made as big of an impression in BeeBee's heart as she had in ours.

I rubbed my fingers along my temples. "No. She's been kidnapped."

Chapter 21

"Kidnapped? By Asnee's father or whoever that whacko is?"

"No. By her mother." My dry tone conveyed my disgust easily enough.

As soon as the nurse mentioned *high-profile*, I knew. Deidra had been in here throwing fits and insisting her daughter wasn't meant to be in a general ICU area; I had no doubt in my mind. The big question was, where would she have her taken? And after that, where was Griff?

There was only one thing for me to do. "Come on," I linked arms with BeeBee and headed back to the parking lot, the double glass doors of the lobby swooshing open as we neared. "We're going to confront the monster."

~

The Mayoral Mansion, as Sam and I liked to call it, where Gregory and Deidra Lowe had moved to when he was first elected mayor, sat just close enough to the private road in the gated community to remain visible, thus the envy of the neighborhood, while still far enough back to require a long, picturesque drive through meticulously maintained landscaping. Not only was it located in a gated community, but the property itself was fitted with a tall wrought iron gate.

A little brick guard shack, smaller than a linen closet really, sat at the entrance to Number 11775 Princeton Drive. I pulled adjacent to the tiny structure and rolled down my window.

"Good afternoon. Do you have an appointment?"

"No," I began, but the intercom crackled back to life and cut me off.

"Entry is by appointment only," the male voice drawled.

"Jerry, it's me. It's Piper." I spoke to the guard, drawing him closer to the window of his booth. "Jerry, you have to let me in there. This is urgent. Trust me, you can let me in. Sam would want you to let me in." I'd been a guest of Sam a couple of times when she had expressly ignored her mother's suggestion that I didn't quite fit the guest list.

The guard dropped his eyes, not meeting my pleading gaze. "Sorry, ma'am. No entry without an appointment."

I hated to resort to this, but I would do whatever it took. "Jerry Kipper, you will let me in this instant or I will never bake a Scrumdiddlyumptious Cake for your wife's birthday again." Jerry Kipper came into the bakery for desserts often enough, but twice a year you could count on him being the first in line. I made a very specific cake just for his wife on her birthday, and her half-birthday

His head snapped up to look at me, stricken. Jerry had come to me fretting that his wife never seemed to like any cakes from the grocery store. He didn't know her favorite flavor, but he'd listed off a whole jumble of desserts she enjoyed at restaurants; from that, I created a custom cake with as many of those flavors as would complement one another and the Scrumdiddlyumptious Cake was born. Jerry's wife bragged on him for months for finding the perfect cake. She loved it so much, he started ordering one six months after her birthday, too.

I crossed my arms and tilted my head. "I'm really sorry, but this is urgent. And important, I promise. So. What'll it be, Jerry?"

Jerry gave a brief nod and tapped a button.

"Brutal," BeeBee whispered from the side of her mouth.

I winked. "But effective," I whispered back.

"Cheer up, Jerry" I spoke louder again, as I threw the truck in gear. "Deidra hates me; tell her it was all my fault and she'll probably forget you were even the one who had to open the gate."

Jerry's lips twitched. He probably knew it was true. I doubt any of Deidra's staff were in the dark concerning her opinion of me. She bemoaned the fact that I had ruined her daughter's chance at wealth and happiness by derailing her bright future by tricking her into working at a "sticky, hole-in-the-wall place baking cookies".

The gate swung backward in an arc, though, unlike the gates at the impound lot, these moved without so much as a squeak; Jerry must keep them greased or oiled or whatever it was you did to gates. I pulled through before he changed his mind.

BeeBee let out a low whistle as I navigated the truck up the long drive and into the circle drive. Three fountains, three, were surrounded by elegant topiary and lush flowers in the grassy area within the paved circle. A short flight of steps took you up to a wrap-around porch that was to die for, complete with mini-bar at one end and jacuzzi around the back corner. Two gray-bricked chimneys rose from the roof; I knew one to be located in the living room and the other from the study. A rounded room on the right, the study would have been my favorite room if it weren't so stark and lifeless; straight-backed chairs, a liquor cabinet, mini-golf, and not a book to be found. The second story boasted a beautiful curved balcony coming from the rounded room on that floor.

I took it as a good sign that we weren't met by the butler with a shotgun or multiple armed security guards. Instead, it was only one guard.

"Uh-oh," BeeBee darted her eyes from the guard to me and back.

"Follow my lead," I told her. "And don't forget the flowers." I stepped out and pocketed my truck keys. As we stepped off the paved drive and onto the path leading to the porch, the guard stepped slightly forward, but not enough to block us. I continued at a steady pace. The sound of gravel crunching behind me was enough to know BeeBee was keeping up.

"Pardon me," I inclined my head to the guard and polished my best southern smile. "Sam's expecting us."

A swift nod his only response, the guard stepped back into the shade of a tall tree. My heart fluttered with relief. It wasn't a lie if Sam was here, and now my hopes soared that she might be, then she would definitely be expecting me to come to find her.

I led BeeBee up the steps and rapped my knuckles on the dark red door. The butler, yes Deidra seriously employed a butler who I believe was Sam's third uncle once removed or something, opened the door. I didn't wait, didn't attempt civility; no begging, no threats. I marched right past the old man with his sleepy expression and headed to the living room first, where I had seen smoke from the chimney.

"Good morning, Deidra," I spoke calmly as I entered the room, forcing myself to assume a relaxed pose and not cross my arms and glare at her.

As wife to the mayor and someone who prided herself on poise, Deidra's only reaction to my surprise visit was a tightening at the mouth and one pristine eyebrow climbing higher than the other in slow motion. The raised eyebrow, it must be a family trait.

"Piper. I wasn't expecting you this morning. I'm afraid I don't have any refreshments to offer." Deidra steepled her fingers together in her lap.

"Don't worry, I won't be long." I smiled. "Just point me to Sam and I'll be on my way."

"Aren't you going to introduce your friend?" Deidra glanced pointedly at BeeBee.

BeeBee stepped forward without hesitation. "I'm BeeBee. I'm also a friend of Sam's and we would like to see her this morning. I need to give her these flowers, too."

"How…lovely," Deidra frowned at the vase of flowers which I had no doubt fell short of her exacting standards.

More than capable of holding her own, BeeBee smiled as if Deidra had just given her an award. "They are lovely, aren't they? I put them together myself and each flower represents healing, renewal, and joy."

"Sam will love them," I said. "Now, where did you say she was again?"

"Sam needs her rest. I will not be answering any of your questions which is obviously more than I can say for the incompetent hospital staff." Deidra stood then, taking two steps toward us. "As you have seen yourself into my home, you may now kindly show yourself out."

"Absolutely," I nodded and turned. "And I will be happy to do so, right after I've seen Sam."

"Stop!" I paid no attention as Deidra continued to shout at me. "I asked you to leave. Where do you think you're going?" The clip-clop of heels sounded as she came after BeeBee and me.

The thing about being a proper lady though was that one never ran; I had no fear that Deidra would even come close to catching me. I considered going up the stairs to Sam's old room but decided to check the guest bedroom on the ground floor instead. If I were a doctor carting around a patient, I would veto stairs.

The guest room door was cracked, no guard posted somewhat to my surprise, and I was delighted to find Sam tucked into the bed when I entered.

"Thank God, you found me," she smiled when BeeBee and I approached. I sat down on the edge of the bed while BeeBee placed the flowers on the nightstand. "Thank you! Those are beautiful." Sam reached out and squeezed BeeBee's hand. "There's a chair in the corner; pull it over here if you want to sit down."

"Never in my life…." Deidra's ranting voice carried into the room, a quick warning before she barged in.

"Mother," Sam sweetened up the word, "thank you so much for bringing my friends. How very thoughtful of you!" She smiled up at a flabbergasted Deidra. "I'm feeling much better already."

I turned my face toward Sam, hiding my smirk from Deidra. Sam had masterfully robbed her mother of speech. Priceless.

"Yes. I'm glad you are feeling better, dear. Still, you need rest. Your friends understood they could only visit with you a few minutes, I'm sure." The ill-concealed ice in her voice left Deidra's meaning clear: we would be leaving soon, one way or another.

"Yes," I nodded at Sam and continued to avoid Deidra's death glare which she must have been giving me by now.

"Yes ma'am," BeeBee added her agreement.

Deidra retreated back to the living room and likely a large glass of brandy. I closed the door softly after she was gone. "When did she move you?" I asked, settling back into a comfortable position on the bed.

"Late last night. She whizzed in on her way to a Ladies Society meeting to ask if I'd scheduled lunch yet. Landon was just leaving and I think seeing him there upset her; the next thing I knew, a nurse was giving me pills in a paper cup. She said the pills were for the headache." Sam's mouth twisted down. "I woke up here."

"You weren't kidding, Piper. She really was kidnapped by her mother."

I nodded at BeeBee. "What was the point though?" I asked aloud.

Sam pointed to an enormous bouquet of red roses on the dresser. They dripped money and screamed impersonal, a bouquet a florist sold twenty times a day probably. "Two motives: first, so she can be the doting mother sacrificing her time to care for the poor, injured, prodigal daughter; second, to try once more to make me see things her way, including a future with 'appropriate' men."

I walked to the dresser and read the card on the obnoxious bouquet aloud. DEAREST SAMANTHA, IT WAS A SHOCK TO HEAR ABOUT YOUR ACCIDENT. I HOPE YOU ARE WELL IN TIME FOR DINNER AT THE END OF JULY. GARRETT HOPSINGER.

"Who is Garrett?" BeeBee wanted to know.

"Never met him," Sam rolled her eyes. "Evidently, he's my date to my father's mayoral dinner."

"The one you had to agree to go to in order for your mother to help get me released from holding in Pierson County?" I knew there couldn't be any other dinners that Sam would willingly attend, but I checked just the same.

"That's right. Along with mandatory, hand-picked date." Sam sighed and closed her eyes. "I foolishly thought once upon a time that she would stop trying to control my life when I was an adult. Obviously, I was wrong."

"She is determined," I agreed.

"That's not the worst part," Sam looked back up at us. "Landon brought me a beautiful flower arrangement that he got from Flo's. Look around, do you see it?"

We both shook our heads in the negative.

"Mother didn't bring it. By now, I'm sure it has been tossed in the trash somewhere in the hospital."

I bit my lip to contain a smile. It would be inappropriate to smile at my friend's distress, but I couldn't help but be happy that something might be developing between her and Landon. It would be interesting to watch.

"She's really something, isn't she?" BeeBee curled her lip in disgust, snapping me out of my own matchmaking fantasy and back to the reality of Deidra's narcissism.

After some questions, we learned that Sam was still being seen by a doctor, her mother's private physician. "He left about an hour ago. He says that I shouldn't be surprised if the headaches come and go for the next several months. So far, the spots have remained clear from my vision and I finally feel awake and alert again. The doctor said those are both good signs that, even if I experience Post-Concussion Syndrome, it will not be severe for me."

I realized that we should be going soon if we wanted to make it to church on time so that I could introduce BeeBee to Pastor Dan. I'd been thinking that she might be able to get a spot at the O Heavenly Day Spa, since the church operated it as part of a relief ministry for abused women, both for rejuvenating treatments or jobs to restore them to a place of independence.

"You're taking me with you, right? That is why you came, a jailbreak?" Sam tugged at my arm.

"I'm going to leave that up to Griff," I told her. "I don't think even I could sneak you out of here with Deidra in the house. She'd probably call the cops on me for something if I even tried. Where is your brother anyway?"

"Don't know. I haven't seen him since yesterday before I was moved."

"Well, if I see him, then I'll let him know to come here and get you."

"Thanks. Thanks for the flowers, BeeBee." Sam waved bye as we left the room. I took a direct path to the front door. No need to experience the pleasure of Deidra's company again if we could help it.

We left the grounds without incident. On the way out, I promised to have some free goodies waiting for Jerry at the bakery the next time that he came in. He nodded, but he still didn't look convinced that he wasn't going to be fired. He kept glancing up the hill at the main house, even while I was speaking to him.

Chapter 22

Miracle of all miracles, we arrived at Sandy Shores Evangelical Church with two minutes to spare before the morning service began. I nearly bumped into Griff as we were heading into the foyer. "Hey stranger," I greeted him. "I tried to call you this morning."

"I know. I've been on the phone all day trying to find Sam. Mother has taken her to a private care facility or something. I was just asking Pastor Dan's wife if anybody had mentioned Deidra bringing Sam to the spa for treatments."

I brought a hand to Griff's shoulder. "I found her. Your mother took her home with her and is having doctors visit the house."

"Are you serious?"

"Yep. BeeBee and I just left there."

"How did you…?" Music began playing and I held up a hand, interrupting Griff's question.

"I'll explain later. Sam wants you to come and take her home. Deidra is basically holding her hostage in the guest bedroom."

Griff rubbed his forehead. "That is crazy. She didn't even like to care for us as sick kids. Why would she insist Sam be there now?"

"She has her own agenda, no doubt. We have to get inside though. The service is starting." I squeezed his arm and then eased through the doors of the sanctuary with BeeBee behind me. Since the praise and worship had already started, everyone was standing up which made it easier to come in unnoticed. I slipped into a row of chairs at the back and let the music flow over me as I caught my breath from the morning's events.

I joined in with the singing, willing my thoughts to clear. Soon, a calm and joy bubbled within me and my smile grew as I sang louder. Though the words were on two different screens up front, BeeBee appeared uncomfortable and watched the crowded room of people. A fleeting thought crossed my mind: I wondered if BeeBee had ever been to church before.

As the choir returned to their seats and the music time ended, Pastor Dan crossed the platform and stopped behind the pulpit. "Good morning brothers and sisters!" Pastor Dan, though quiet in person, was always excited during his sermon. "What a fine and beautiful day God has given us."

"Amen," chorused several of the front row individuals.

"Let us rejoice and be glad in this day." Pastor Dan prayed, quoting part of Psalm 118:24, followed by giving praise to the Creator and remarking on several specific things he was joyful about today. Afterward, he launched right into his sermon on freedom. "With Independence Day right around the corner," he said at one point, "one should consider the hard-won freedom. But I'm not talking about freedom of religion, freedom of speech, or freedom from other countries. I want to look at what the Bible tells us of the ultimate freedom. Freedom from sin, freedom from chains, freedom from the wrath of God that we cannot win, we cannot earn, we cannot write for ourselves. This freedom is given only through Jesus Christ."

The sermon was poignant, there were shouts of agreement and clapping, men and women alike stepping out to pray at the altar. Pastor Dan closed the sermon reminding us the cost of our freedom as believers, reading John 3:16 *For God so loved the world, that He gave His only Son, that whoever believes in Him shall be saved.* For myself, it was a reminder that I didn't rejoice in my freedom in Christ as often as it warranted; I didn't always value it as precious as the price that was paid for it. BeeBee, I noticed, brushed away a stray tear or two.

After the close of the service, I stayed put with BeeBee in our seats as the rest of the congregation trickled out. Some went alone, some were in families, many others clustered together in groups of friends all moving slowly as one big unit toward the double-door exits on the right and left sides of the back wall.

Gladys caught sight of us as she was on her way to the exit and scooted in to sit with us. That turned out to be a good thing; I was able to tell her not to bother stopping back by the hospital to see Sam since she was no longer a patient there.

"Has that woman ever had her brain examined?" Gladys asked about Deidra.

"No, doctors have been too busy searching for a heart all of these years," I joked.

"Where's Griff?" she asked.

"Gone to break Sam out of confinement. He left right after closing prayers to go to Deidra's place and check on Sam."

At last, the long line of people leaving dwindled to only two or three. "Would you mind opening up the bakery with Victoria if I'm running late?" I asked Gladys. "I want to introduce BeeBee to Pastor Dan and Nora." We had been opening the bakery at one on Sundays lately, and quite the after-church crowd had been frequenting it. It was a good compromise; we still got part of the day off, yet the bakery still sold plenty of goodies in the afternoon to make opening worth it.

"I don't mind at all," Gladys gave BeeBee a hug. "You'll just love Pastor Dan. Everybody does."

~

Nora and Pastor Dan had insisted we join them for coffee and tea in the pastor's office. It was snug fitting four of us in the small room, but cozy and full of life. Framed photos decorated the walls, interspersed with crosses and Bible verse plaques; the bookshelves were bulging with volumes stacked every-which-way. "Are you sure we can't get you anything to eat?" Nora asked for the second time, looking closely at BeeBee.

BeeBee pulled a chocolate from the candy bowl on the desk. "No thanks, this is fine." She looked at her hands as she began to unwrap the silver foil from around the treat. "I thought that what you had to say this morning was really interesting, sir." She glanced at Pastor Dan and ducked her glance again.

"Thank you, but it isn't just me saying it. God gives us the promise of freedom and forgiveness in the Bible," Pastor Dan smiled wide. "Would you like to read some of them?"

"I guess so, yes." BeeBee leaned forward in the chair as Pastor Dan opened his thick Bible up and took her through what to me were the familiar passages of the Romans Road, several scriptures in the book of Romans that explained about salvation. As for BeeBee, her eyes widened more with each new verse until I feared she was going to strain them.

When BeeBee didn't say anything after they were through, Pastor Dan reached around behind him and pulled a thinner leather book from the shelf. "Here. I'd like you to take this Bible and read some more whenever you want to. Nora or I am always around here somewhere and would be happy to answer any questions."

"Okay. Thank you," BeeBee grasped the Bible tightly and wiggled in her chair, seemingly unable to get comfortable.

"You know," I took a sip of iced tea, "I was wondering if there were any openings or perhaps a need for an extra set of hands at the spa?"

"Oh? Are you looking to get out of the bakery?" Nora asked, eyes wide with a look of surprise.

"No, not for me. For BeeBee. She worked at a massage establishment," I ignored BeeBee nearly choking on her candy next to me, and forged on with my idea. "I thought, with as busy as the O Heavenly Day Spa stays, there might be work for her there?"

"How old are you, BeeBee?" Nora handed her a napkin. "If you don't mind my asking, of course. You just look so young."

"I'm seventeen."

Pastor Dan shook his head. "Unfortunately, the policy says we can't hire anyone for a massage therapist position under the age of eighteen. When is your birthday?"

BeeBee washed the last of her chocolate down with a drink. "In December," she answered.

"If you'll come to the spa in November and get an application, I'd be happy to go with you when you turn it in." Pastor Dan smiled, wide and warm. "I have a little pull with the hiring department, you know." He chuckled.

"Darling, I don't want to cut our chat short but you do remember you have to leave for the jail soon, right?" Nora glanced at the bracelet on her arm and I noticed it had a small clock charm on it.

"We're sorry for taking up so much of your time," I stood to leave.

"Don't be sorry. It was a pleasure to meet you BeeBee," Pastor Dan shook her hand. "Don't forget about that application, and I hope to see you plenty before your birthday. Piper, we'll be by for some more delicious desserts soon."

"Sounds great, Pastor." I fell into step beside Nora as we spilled out into the hallway. "Nora, did you say Dan has to go to the jail?"

"Yes. It's visiting day on Sunday and my dear Dan tries to go at least once a month to see some of the folks who don't get visitors. He brings some little encouragement and offers free Bibles as well."

"I see. Thanks for sharing. Y'all have a wonderful afternoon." I hugged Nora and Pastor Dan. They stood holding hands in the doorway, waving as we left the church parking lot.

~

BeeBee went into Flo's, while I hurried inside the bakery. Gladys had her hands full with the after-church crowd and I took over handing out goodies while she took payments. When we finally hit a lull and everyone was seated, I swiped the screen on my phone and opened my internet browser. A quick search showed me the information I wanted; Pierson County Jail was also open for visitation this afternoon until five pm.

My phone rang. "Hey," I answered it. "I was just about to call you."

"Hey yourself," Griff said. "Before I forget, I got a call from Sheriff Kent a few minutes ago."

"Did they catch the guy?" I squeezed the phone a little tighter.

"No. They found a white Mercedes abandoned, flat tire, on a back road not far from where you and Sam were run off the highway."

My heart sank. The partial license plate from the Mercedes was the only solid lead the police had. It was beginning to look like the bad guy was going to get away with murder. "Any sign of the dark car that ran us off the road?" I doubted it but had to ask.

"Nope." I could hear the frustration in Griff's voice. "He says with no make, model, or plate number that they have nothing to go on to even look for it." There was a short pause before Griff tried to change the subject and cheer me up. "I got Sam home, safe and sound."

"Good!" I smiled, though he couldn't see me. "What did it take this time?"

A low chuckle escaped as Griff answered. "Sam told Mother that if she didn't let her leave, she would start writing the doctor notes that she was being held hostage."

"Good for her."

"Didn't you say you were calling me about something?" Griff asked. "Let me guess, you miss me already?"

"Ha," I laugh. "Yes, but I'm calling for a different reason. How would you feel about a little road trip to Pierson County this afternoon?" I explained my plan. Griff grudgingly agreed to pick me up in fifteen minutes. "At least I called you," I told him.

"True. Maybe there's hope for you yet," he joked.

I told Gladys the plan while I waited for Griff.

"Hmm," she ran a finger across her chin thoughtfully. "It might work." She grabbed a small plastic to-go container and put a sampling of six different desserts in it. Handing it over to me, she said, "Take these just in case though. More flies with honey and all that – sugar is probably even better than honey."

"Thanks, Gladys." Minutes later, Griff arrived to pick me up as promised. As we drove, panicked thoughts assaulted my mind. *Did I really want to do this? Go back into that jail? Sit across from Regina and ask for her help, when not long ago she would have killed me or sold me to other traffickers if given the chance?* The thoughts tempted me to abandon my plan. But, deep down, I knew I would regret it if I didn't at least try. I had to do this.

Chapter 23

Griff parked in the visitor lot of Pierson County Jail. I stared out the window at the ugly tan brick building. A shiver coursed through me and I gave an involuntary shudder. I did not want to be here.

"Are you sure you want to do this?" Griff asked.

"Of course," I lied. Not one single part of me felt good about this. Still, the determination lingered.

"We could grab a late lunch instead. Nobody would blame you for not going inside."

"It's fine. Regina might know something and if she does, I want to find out." I grabbed the door handle. "I'll be okay, really."

"I still think I should go in with you." Griff frowned, tucking a strand of hair behind my ear.

"And I appreciate that," I told him. "I think that Regina will be more likely to talk if she doesn't feel ganged up on though. I'll be back soon."

I forced myself to walk up the steps to the jail's main entrance, not looking back at Griff waiting patiently in the truck lest I give up and run back to him. I cringed as my mind played my time in a holding cell over on a loop; the smells, even in memory, made me nearly gag. When Pastor Dan mentioned visiting at the jail it had spurred this crazy thought in me that Regina might be hurting for visitors. Perhaps she'd had time to think about her actions; maybe she even regretted them. If so, she might know something about the man who kept trying to kill me.

I noticed there were not many other names listed as I signed in on the visitor's list.

"License or other valid ID?" the officer behind the desk held out a hand expectantly.

"Here you go." I fished my driver's license out of my purse and handed it to him. I was grateful Sheriff Kent had called in to get me added to the Approved Visitor Roster while Griff and I were on the way over.

"Have a seat in the waiting area," the officer instructed, returning my license. "You'll need to leave your purse in a locker. Here's a list of items allowed in the visitation room."

I took the slip of paper; it didn't need to be large because the list it contained was minimal: ID, glasses (medical), change or dollar bills. *So much for bribing her with cookies,* I thought. Griff and I would just have to eat those on the way home. I placed my purse in a locker and took the key from the door. It would be stupid for someone to steal inside of a jail, but I wasn't taking any chances.

After sitting for about twenty minutes, I saw a stream of people exit a side door. Another officer, a young female, brought up the rear of the line. "Next visitation group," she called.

I fell into line with others from the waiting area and we were led to a large open room with several small plastic tables and chairs. Most of the tables were occupied by one inmate. I searched the faces and finally spotted Regina.

"You." Regina bit out the word, crossing her arms over her chest.

"Me," I smiled but faltered at her icy stare. This wasn't going to be easy; darn, I wish I had those cookies. Might as well cut to the chase. "Listen, I was hoping to get some information from you. If it helps, it might even look good to the D.A. at trial."

"I have nothing to say to you."

"Just hear me out. It's not like you have anywhere else to be." Oops. Maybe not the honeyed approach that Gladys recommended. "Please," I added.

Regina stared.

Right then, here we go. "Did you send someone to kill me?"

"Excuse me?"

"There's a guy that has been following me, and my friends, bugging our vehicles. He tried to shoot me, then tried to have me killed in a car wreck. Did you send him after me?"

"You come in here, tell me if I talk to you it could help me out, and now you're trying to get me to confess to conspiracy to murder?" Regina shook her head. "You must be a bigger idiot than I thought, sweetheart. I still can't believe you were let go after they found you with the murder weapon at that stupid company retreat."

I ignored her and kept trying. "He's Asian, lots of demon tattoos kind of like Asnee; oh, and he said Asnee was his son."

Surprise flashed in Regina's eyes, her brows lifting slightly. Then she quirked her lips up and shrugged. "Don't know. Never heard of him."

"Yes, you have, you recognized that description. I saw it."

Regina pursed her lips.

I pushed on. "You know him. Do you know where he lives or hangs out? Places he might be? He drove a white Mercedes but he ditched it…."

At the mention of the car, Regina bolted forward in the chair. "What did you say?" I scooted back. She looked like she might strangle me at any moment. I slid my eyes around the room, trying not to turn away from Regina, and was disappointed to see the guard was on the opposite side of the visitation area. Hopefully still close enough to save me if Regina lost it. Gulp.

"What did you say he was driving?" she demanded.

"A white Mercedes."

The snarl that crossed her face was downright scary.

"I can't believe that no good son-of-a…what does he think he's doing, driving my car? My car! The nerve. And you say he abandoned it?" Her fingernails were all but digging into the table in front of her as she balled them in and out of fists.

Yes! I did a little cheer on the inside. A hot topic, a pressure point I could use. I couldn't pass up on this opportunity. "Is that your car? Wow, that sucks. Police have it now. Like I say, first, he tried to kill me in a car wreck and then he ditched your car on some little back road. Too hot to drive, I'm sure." I tilted my head up at the ceiling for a moment. "You know…" I let the sentence linger. "I think he even left the keys in it." I mean, I wasn't sure but he probably did; Regina didn't have to know that. "I'm surprised it wasn't stolen before the police took it."

Regina was pissed. Boiling over mad. I thought at any minute steam would rise from the tight bun on her head and out both ears, just like on all of those cartoons. Maybe I'd gone a little too far.

"It seems kind of unfair that he's out there, joyriding in your car, while you're stuck in here. He did kill someone, too, yet he gets no punishment. The police don't even know his name."

"Susumu Takumi."

"I'm sorry, what?"

"His name. Susumu Takumi." Regina repeated it slowly.

"Wait. I wasn't ready." Gosh, I wish you were allowed to bring a phone or pen and paper in here. "Can you spell that?"

Silence.

"Okay, guess I'll just look it up." *Susumu. Susumu.* I tried repeating it in my head. I needed to get out of here and tell someone. "One last thing. Any idea where we might find him?"

"You'll tell the police I helped?" She folded her arms across her chest again.

"I will. I don't know what they might do, but I will tell them."

"And you won't testify against me?"

I paused. We really needed this information. I didn't want to be looking over one shoulder for the rest of my life. I knew I had to do the right thing though; there was no way I wasn't going to testify, I had already decided that passing out or no passing out I was going to get in that box tomorrow and share Regina's involvement in the trafficking, the abduction of myself and my friends, and the incriminating voicemail confession. I could lie. I opened my mouth, "No deal. I have to testify. I will be honest and I will answer with any information I know. But I will also tell them you were cooperative if we are able to catch what's his name."

"Susumu," she rolled her eyes at me like I was an idiot. "Fine. I had to try. I figured you were too much of a goody-two-shoes."

Goody-two-shoes…that's another one I'm going to have to look up. When did people start saying these oddball things anyway?

Regina spoke again and I shook my thoughts away. Time to listen.

Chapter 24

I rapped hard on the truck window and laughed when Griff jerked upright. I caught him sleeping.

"What'd you do that for?" he asked, rubbing his eyes.

"Because I can," I stuck my tongue out at him.

Griff cranked the truck. "Did you learn anything?"

"You better believe I did." I had more information than I expected from Regina. Scary information.

"Okay. Where to now?"

"We need to talk to Sheriff Kent. Quickly."

I called to let the sheriff know to expect us. During the long drive back to Seashell Bay, I shared what I learned with Griff. By the time we got to the sheriff's department, I was tired, but I prepared to repeat it all anyway.

"Shoot!"

"What's the matter?" Griff and I were halfway up the walkway.

"I forgot to ask Regina if she knew who might be driving the dark-colored car."

"You mean the one that actually ran you off the road after you made her think someone used her car to do it?" He laughed.

"Listen," I wagged my finger at him. "I got us a ton of information, did I not?"

"I'm not judging." Griff held the glass door open for me. "Ladies first."

The secretary escorted us immediately into Sheriff Kent's private office.

"Any incidents on your drive?" Sheriff Kent shook both of our hands but directed the question to Griff.

"Not one."

"Good. Good." We all sat down and the sheriff leaned his elbows on the large desk between us and him. "Tell me Miss Rivers. Did you catch anything on this little fishing expedition of yours?"

"A whopper," I told him. "According to Regina, the man who is after me is named Susumu Takumi." I had looked it up on the drive and found similar first and last names, though for different people. "Susumu is the leader of a small group of Yakuza."

"Come again?"

"Yakuza. Basically, if I understood her correctly, they are Japanese gangsters." Scary ones, I thought about the articles I had skimmed.

"What in the world would Japanese gangsters be doing in Alabama?" Sheriff Kent picked up a pencil, twirling it between his fingers.

"I don't know. Regina didn't say where she met them. Honestly, I was lucky she told me as much as she did."

"Understood. Go on."

As Sheriff Kent nodded for me to continue, I thought back over my conversation with Regina. "She says besides Susumu and Asnee, there were three other men that she knew of. They were brought on board as muscle and transport."

"We can assume one of the other three was the man Susumu shot at the construction site," Griff spoke up.

I agreed. "Probably. Similar tattoos. The tattoos have symbolism for the gang, though obviously, we can't go around assuming everyone with tattoos is a bad person. The Yakuza have very specific tattoos with meanings associated, so it is still something to keep an eye out for."

The sheriff now used the pencil to jot down notes as I spoke. When he looked up from the notepad, I continued. "Regina gave me two locations where you might find him."

"You didn't want to start with that bit?" Sheriff Kent chastised. "Where at?" His hand hovered over the notepad, waiting.

"Besuto Auto Repair or Asian Garden Restaurant." The former was located on the long stretch of highway between Seashell Bay and Lion's Cove; the latter over in Lion's Cove.

"Asian Garden is out of my county," Sheriff Kent commented what we already knew. "I can take a run at Besuto Auto Repair though."

"If he spooks, Regina said Susumu can become a ghost pretty easily." My warning earned a frown from the sheriff. "I'm not trying to tell you how to do your job. I'm only trying to help and give you all the information I can. I need this guy behind bars so I can sleep at night."

"Fair enough," he said. "I'll put an unmarked car on Besuto tonight and tomorrow."

"Thanks." I smiled, a weight lifting off my shoulders. "Do you think you could get word to Officer Campbell about Asian Garden? He isn't too fond of me and I doubt he would listen."

"I'll give him a call if we catch this so-called Japanese gangster."

"Great." We shook hands again with the sheriff and he buzzed the secretary to escort us out. Back at the truck, Griff asked what was next on our agenda.

"Honestly, I really need to get back to the bakery. At the way we've been going, the town is going to think that Sam and I sold it to Gladys."

"You need to eat something," Griff frowned. "Besides cookies."

I closed my mouth again; he cut me off before I could tell him I would grab something to eat at the bakery. Better step up my game if I'm getting that predictable. *Plus,* I thought about the new clothes we bought this weekend, *he's probably right. I might need to eat something besides a load of sugar every so often or I'll be buying bigger size clothes next time.* "I will agree to eat whatever you decide, on one condition."

"What's that?"

"We order it to-go and you drop me and my food off at the bakery. I'd feel better if you went and checked on Sam."

"That's fine by me."

Soon, I was sitting on a stool, crunching happily on asparagus and steak from a little plastic box. "Victoria, do you want some?" I really should have called and asked if they wanted us to pick them up food; since I didn't, the least I could do was share.

"No, but thanks anyway. Some fancy chef guy delivered us some sandwiches. They were fancy too, the sandwiches; I think he called them Croque Monsieur."

Interesting, Chef Fabio is making deliveries for Gladys.

I finished up my meal, scarfing down the last large bites of steak in a very unladylike fashion, and tossed the container in the trash. After washing and drying my hands, I gathered an assortment of ingredients.

"What are you making?" Victoria wanted to know.

"No idea," I told her honestly. "I just need to mix something, create, forget about the last few days and let my brain run on auto-pilot for a bit."

She nodded. "I get that. It's kind of like when my Aunt Sophie decides to re-organize her bookstore. She spends days un-shelving, sorting, stacking, and re-shelving books and when I asked why, she told me that it's like hitting a reset button for her mood or something like that."

"Exactly!" I pour melted butter into a bowl. "Your aunt sounds like a smart lady. Wait, she doesn't own Babbling Books here in town, does she?"

"Yeah. Have you been in there?"

I scooped sugar into the butter mixture. "Once or twice. I've gotten used to ordering things online, and that includes books, but I remember finding an awesome cookbook section in her store now that you've mentioned it."

Victoria grinned. "Don't tell my Aunt Sophie that. Books are her babies."

"Noted." The microwave beeped. I pulled a small bowl of melted chocolate chips out and poured them into the butter-sugar mixture. Next came the batch of dry ingredients. While I incorporated those into my cookie dough, I watched Victoria check the oven timer and bend over to peer inside. "What's baking?" I asked.

"Coconut Macaroons." She paced the kitchen, always coming back to look inside the oven.

"First time baking them?" I asked.

She stopped short and spun to face me. "How'd you know? Oh my gosh! Are they burning? Did I mess them up?"

My head fell back in laughter. "No. I'm sure they are fine. You seem a little nervous, that's all."

"Ah. Okay. I guess I don't have to look in on them every three seconds for the oven to bake right, huh?"

"No. Why don't you make yourself some coffee and relax." Sam and I had been stocking more decaf ever since coming back from our catering gig to find Victoria zooming around in an espresso-induced frenzy. "It looks like those still have six more minutes; you will wear yourself out. How long did you set the timer?"

"Eighteen minutes," she ran her fingers across her forehead. "You're right. I'll sit down a minute."

"The macaroons will be great. Don't doubt yourself, remember."

While Victoria brewed a small cup of coffee, I looked back at my dough. It was missing something. I wandered into the panty and spun in a slow, slow circle. Just looking. Thinking. Aha! I grabbed the hazelnuts and extra-dark chocolate chips off of a shelf.

Victoria sat on a stool, her knee bouncing rapidly. I talked about my cookie dough to distract her. Her knee stopped bouncing. She listened, asked questions, and sipped her coffee. Then the oven timer buzzed. The poor girl jolted up like she'd been electrocuted. Her coffee overturned, dark liquid fingering out in every direction.

I took pity on her as she froze, her gaze darting between the mess and the oven. "I've got the spill. You get your macaroons."

Delicious coconut smells enveloped the room as Victoria opened the oven door wide.

I soaked coffee up into a dish rag and tossed it in a bin of other dirty ones. I'd need to take those home to wash tonight; it was yet another thing that I had neglected, being so focused on the trial and distracted by the attempts on my life. Good excuses, yes, but guilt gnawed at my insides. The Ooey Gooey Goodness Bakery was my dream; I loved our business and it deserved proper care. I intended to do better from now on.

Gladys poked her head through the swinging door. "What's Sam's favorite Fourth of July cookie?"

"Red, White, and Blueberry Truffles," I said automatically. "Why?" It was too late. The swinging door swung slowly to a stop. Gladys had popped out before I could ask the question.

"Odd," I murmured to myself. Pulling my phone from my apron pocket, I checked for messages. Nothing from Griff or Sam. "I wonder what that was all about."

"Earth to Piper."

"Sorry, what?"

Victoria waved me over to the counter. "Do these Coconut Macaroons look right to you?"

"They look perfect." I leaned closer, noticing that besides the tray of perfectly toasted coconut confections were four grayish-black blobs. I pointed to them. "Except these. These look strange."

"Oh yeah. I used food coloring on those to see if we could include them for the Fourth of July goodies menu."

"Gotcha. Well, I think you should use a little less food coloring, maybe only one drop, and they should brighten up."

Victoria rubbed her hands together. "So. Are you going to taste one with me?"

"Absolutely!" I put my hand on her wrist as she reached for the tray. "Um, but maybe not the black ones. Just a regular macaroon for me please."

"Yeah, they do look kind of terrible, don't they?"

"Completely." I laughed, then bit into my macaroon. Whimpered. "This is excellent. Moist, amazingly tender, slightly crunchy on the coconut covering the outside." I swallowed the remaining half and licked my thumb and finger of the sweet goodness. "Victoria, did I mention you are hired forever...whenever you want to work here."

She threw her arms around me. "Thank you. Thank you for giving Millie and I a shot at working here, and for keeping us longer than that first weekend. I've had so much fun and now I know more than ever that I want to apply to the Culinary Institute of America. I wasn't sure I would be good enough, but you make me feel like I can do anything. You've taught me so much and I want to learn everything. I want to learn styles from different countries, I want to learn about rare ingredients, all of it."

I watched the excitement light up her entire face. Joy coursed through me. I had wanted to encourage Victoria. I had worked to increase her confidence. But to see her passion and her plans bubbling out of her, to hear her say that I helped inspire her to go for her dreams, that made me incredibly happy, proud, and honored all at the same time. To make a difference in someone's life, there isn't anything like that feeling.

My cookies baked quickly. They were ooey gooey goodness for sure! "What should we call these?" I asked Victoria as I handed her a warm cookie to try.

"Let's see." She chewed thoughtfully. "Chocolate with more chocolate and nuts. Maybe something like Chocolate Doubles? Double Downs?"

I snapped my fingers. "How about Double Deluxe Cookies?"

"That's good. Yeah, let's call them that. Great job, can I have another one?" Victoria held out one hand while using the other to shovel in the rest of her cookie. A girl after my own heart.

Victoria volunteered to load the dishwasher so that I could go up front to stock the display case and talk to Gladys.

"Have you heard from anyone next door today?" I thumbed in the direction of Flo's Flowers as I bent over to unload cookies onto the shelves.

"Not a peep, though that isn't surprising."

"Why not?"

"With the number of flower and cookie promo coupons I've seen today, Flo probably hasn't stopped moving all day long. The girls, too." Gladys fanned a small stack of redeemed coupons in front of my face.

"Those are all from today?" I held the stack, flicking through. There had to be more than thirty.

"Every last one," she started to stick them back in the register.

"Good grief! Here let me keep those. I need to take those home with me and figure out a schedule for baking all of the requested Fourth of July specials." I didn't know if I should be excited or overwhelmed; the promotion idea taking off so well surprised me. I considered the short amount of time before the big day. Five. In five days, it would be Independence Day. Yikes!

"There's Millie now." Gladys nudged me and pointed to the door.

The bell jingled as the girl sped inside.

"Piper! I'm glad you're here." Millie hugged Gladys and me on either side of her. "You have got to call Sam. Right now!"

Chapter 25

I grabbed Millie by the forearms. "What happened? What's wrong?"

"Nothing is wrong. Everything is excellent."

"Then why the urgency?"

Millie bounced up and down on her toes. "We need to tell her to make an appointment at the salon, fast. Over 150 orders have been placed for Independence Day Arrangements!" She squealed.

Gladys shifted, looking between Millie and me. "I don't understand what that has to do with Sam getting her nails done."

"Not her nails," I said. "Her hair. Sam made a deal that if over 150 orders were placed during the Fourth of July Sale, she would dye her hair 'patriotic' before the parade."

"Patriotic?"

"Mm-hmm. That's what she said."

"Well, what are we waiting for? Get Sam on the phone." Gladys circled her hands at me, hurrying me along.

I pulled my phone from the apron pocket. "Hey," I decided to call Griff first.

"Hey, yourself. Is everything okay?"

It crossed my mind that we all really had to find some new, safer hobbies if we each thought something might be wrong at all times. "Yep. Everything is excellent," I borrowed Millie's words. "I was calling to talk to Sam actually, but I wanted to check with you first and see how she's been doing."

Griff let out a sigh and I could practically see him rubbing tired eyes. "She's been struggling with the headaches more this afternoon. Too much going on, I think. I can go check, but I would guess she's resting. She turned all the lights off and put half the pillows from her bed on the couch. When I left to come outside earlier, she was curled up and half asleep already."

I heard the scrape of chair legs. "Griff, just peek inside. Please, don't wake her if she is asleep. It can wait until tomorrow."

He mumbled agreement and I waited for a few moments in the quiet. Then his voice came back on the line. "Yeah, she's out like a light."

"Good. Maybe she'll feel better tomorrow. Listen, BeeBee and I are going to my apartment tonight."

"I don't...."

"No, no arguing. Sam needs rest. You need to keep an eye on her way more than on me."

Griff snorted. "Not sure about that."

"We will be okay. The cops are staking out Susumu's hangouts. Court will be over tomorrow. I'll even let you pick me up and drive me to the trial if Sam is still doing fine in the morning." I smiled, imagining Griff rubbing the back of his neck and trying to think of a way to convince me to stay at Sam's place again.

"Lock your doors," Griff put his serious voice on, obviously deciding to save the arguments for a bigger issue.

"I will."

"Call me if you need me."

"I promise." It was funny how he'd gone from my best friend's brother to super-protective boyfriend and we'd only had one official date. It was also funny that I didn't mind a bit.

Millie, though disappointed we couldn't tell Sam the good news right away, was happy to hear she was home and doing okay. She promised to let Flo and BeeBee know. "We will just pray those headaches will disappear soon," she said with a sharp nod and a bob of her long ponytail before spinning and marching back out the front door.

"Speaking of Sam," I turned back to Gladys. "Why did you need to know her favorite cookie flavor?"

"Not a favorite cookie, favorite Fourth of July cookie," Gladys corrected me.

"Right. What was that all about?" I asked, but Gladys only shrugged. I caught her smiling as she turned away. "Tell me, c'mon. You know you want to."

"If you insist." Gladys waggled her eyebrows. "Guess who ordered cookies for our Samantha?"

"Who?"

"Landon!" Gladys shouted, causing several customers to look up from their tables. She kept going, not paying them any attention. "Landon ordered two dozen of those truffles you said Sam likes. With a discount coupon. That means he bought her flowers, too!"

"He did. Buy flowers I mean; I saw them when Sam was at the hospital but her mother left them behind when she took Sam from there."

"That horrid woman. Why doesn't Sam just disown her or something?" Gladys went back to the cash register mumbling to herself.

"Sam isn't the only person who got a delivery from what I hear," I sidled up next to Gladys and spoke quietly.

Her eyes widened. "Who? Who?"

"You."

"What?" Confusion settled over her features.

"That's right. I know about your fancy lunch delivery." I teased, smirking as Gladys's mouth rounded into an O. "So. When do we get to meet Mr. Fancy Chef again?"

Saved by a customer, Gladys turned and smiled sweetly at a young couple holding hands. "What can we get for you two today?" she asked them.

Closing time came not too much later. I had given up teasing Gladys; it would be more fun another time when Sam would be there to help. I sent a text to Flo asking if they were finishing up for the evening and told her to bring the crew into the kitchen for a snack before we all went home.

Five minutes later, we all gathered in the large kitchen which felt smaller with six people in it.

"What are we taste-testing tonight?" Millie asked.

I uncovered the two platters of ooey gooey goodness in the center of the island and everyone moved in a bit closer.

I tilted one tray up to show. "Double Deluxe Cookies."

"And," Victoria did the honors on her tray of tiny desserts, flourishing a hand around them. "Mini Cherry-Limeade Pies."

Chapter 26

I flipped on the light in the hall as BeeBee and I entered my apartment. I grabbed the fanny pack off the side table when I put my keys down, intending to take it to my room. This time I made it to the living room before tossing it on the coffee table.

Both desserts had been a success, though Flo wasn't fond of the fizzing candy in the Mini Cherry-Limeade Pies. I smiled, thinking of everyone's face when the candy registered on their tongues, their brains taking a minute to catch up. Victoria had asked me if it was okay to keep the ingredients secret and see what the reactions were; that was the perfect thing about using your friends as guinea pigs – they never stayed mad forever – so I told her I was perfectly fine with that plan.

"Thanks for letting me stay, Piper." BeeBee plopped her bag on the floor by the couch. "You have a cute apartment." She followed me into the kitchen. "Maybe I can get one like it after I've been working a little bit."

"Maybe so. But don't worry about that right now. Sam and I are happy to have you until you get on your feet. I'm sorry that I don't have a spare room for you, but the couch is pretty comfy."

"It's cool."

"Help yourself to anything in the kitchen or fridge," I opened the refrigerator and stared at the mostly bare shelves. "Not that you have a lot of options. Looks like I have water and some about to expire milk."

BeeBee laughed. "I'm good, but thanks. Do you mind if I use your shower? I feel like I have plant juice all over me from my lessons with Flo and Millie on cutting and arranging the flowers."

"Go right ahead." I led BeeBee through my bedroom, clean thankfully, to the bathroom. "Use my shampoo, soap, all of it. There are towels and wash rags in this cabinet." I opened the door below the sink.

"Perfect."

I pulled some extra blankets from my closet and took them to the living room. I didn't know how warm or cool BeeBee liked to sleep at night, but I hoped she would be comfortable. I relaxed onto the couch and picked up the remote, figuring I would flip channels while I waited for her to get out of the shower.

My eyelids grew heavy and I stretched, settling down further into the couch until I was lying on my side. Headlights flickered through the closed curtains of the living room window, the one that faced the parking lot. I smiled as I remembered Griff spending the entire night sitting outside watching over me. My eyes drifted shut again.

Seconds later, or what felt like seconds, loud bursts of noise startled me wide awake. Automatically, I clutched at the remote driving the volume button down as far as it would go. The noise came again, and this time I flopped to the floor as bullets whizzed through my living room window. Glass in a picture frame on the wall shattered and crashed to the couch, bouncing off to land near my leg. *BeeBee! Must find BeeBee!* My brain screamed at me. I wanted nothing more than to cover my ears and hide behind something. The noise assaulted my ears. I crawled across the floor, sliding on my stomach, not daring to lift my head more than an inch. If BeeBee were in the shower, she might not hear the shooting. If she was out of the shower, she might come rushing right into the line of fire. My cell phone peeked out at me from beneath the coffee table where I dropped it when I dozed off. I slid it to me. Opened my contacts. Kept crawling. Dialed. Crawled.

"911 speaking. What is your emergency?"

"Shooting. Someone is shooting at me. 102 West Haven Apartments, Camden Drive. Hurry." I kept the line open, but nothing the woman on the other end said penetrated the pounding of my blood in my ears. And sirens. I heard sirens. That must be the fastest response time in recorded history. Still, I kept crawling. Once I reached the hall, I came to my feet and ran, bent as low as humanly possible, until I reached my bedroom. BeeBee reached the doorway at the same moment. She stumbled over me and we crashed to the floor. Everything went quiet.

"What in the world is going on?" BeeBee asked, fingernails digging into my arms. "I heard so much noise."

"Shooting. Are you hurt?" I looked over her as we struggled upright and leaned against the wall. Her caramel hair dripped puddles onto the floor. Her pajamas were damp. She must have just gotten out of the shower, I surmised.

"No. Who is shooting? Shooting here? Are you okay?"

Down the hall, my front door began to rattle. I huddled closer to BeeBee, trying to shield her behind me. Two rapid bangs, the door shuddered. I towed BeeBee back into my bedroom and closed the door. Wood splintered and another crash sounded from the hall.

Footsteps banged out a steady beat on the floor.

Someone was in my home.

Chapter 27

"Piper?"

I let out a breath and slumped against the door in relief.

"Piper? BeeBee?" the voice called again.

Opening the bedroom door, BeeBee and I stepped cautiously into the hall. Landon stood beside a uniformed police officer, the two of them barely fitting side-by-side in my tiny entry.

"We're okay," my voice shook.

"Ma'am, paramedics are almost here. They'll want to look you both over, just in case." The officer leaned through the kitchen doorway then gestured inside. "Why don't you come sit down in here and I'll get your statements wrapped up."

I tiptoed through the mess that was my home. Sheetrock dust and shards of glass littered the living room floor, and I stumbled as I walked past the doorway. Bullet holes in the walls made me dizzy. I swayed. My breath came in jerky gasps.

"Come sit. Come on." Landon led me slowly to the kitchen table, BeeBee just behind us. Someone put a glass of water in front of me and I gulped it down, pressing the cool cup to my forehead a moment after. "The shooters?" I asked, sitting the glass down.

Landon and the police officer exchanged a look. I gripped the edge of the table, fearing the worst. "They got away?" I hated the fear, the desperation in my voice.

"They're dead," the officer said bluntly.

BeeBee leaned back and rubbed a hand across her forehead, her posture moving from tense to relaxed.

"Do you, do you have an identity yet?" I crossed my fingers under the table that it would be Susumu, that this nightmare would be over.

"My partner is working the scene now. I came to make sure there were no...that nobody was hurt." He patted me awkwardly on the shoulder. "I'm going to leave you here with this young man until the paramedics arrive."

Long strides carried him quickly from my kitchen. I listened for the door, then remembered it would have to be replaced. "Looks like we'll be house-crashing on Sam after all."

BeeBee smiled. "Yep. It would seem so."

"I still don't understand how the police arrived so quickly. And you," I turned to Landon. "What are you doing here?"

We were interrupted by the arrival of two paramedics. Landon explained, while BeeBee and I had our vitals checked and answered questions, that Griff had sent him to keep watch for the night.

"Of course, he did." I rolled my eyes.

The paramedics determined we were fine, warning that shock might begin to settle in later. They told us to watch for the signs such as rapid breathing, erratic pulse, cool skin, dizziness and so on. With nothing more to do, they left.

"Yeah," Landon pulled out a chair and sat down once they were gone. "He said the sheriff would be busy keeping an eye on that auto shop place. Wanted to know somebody was keeping an eye on you, but he felt it best not to leave Sam completely alone for a few more days." He rapped his knuckles on the table. "He's going to kill me when I tell him I fell asleep for a few minutes though. Dozed right off, otherwise, maybe I would have realized the shooters were watching your apartment."

"How could you have known?" BeeBee frowned.

"I never saw them pull up, so, when I woke, I assumed that car parked under your window was empty; just another resident. All the lights were off. When the headlights came on, I thought it strange that I hadn't seen anybody approach the car, then suddenly guns appeared out the window and they started shooting your place. I dialed the police right away and they told me not to get involved."

I placed a hand on my chest, imagining how scary the scene in the parking lot must have been. Knowing we were inside. "I'm glad you didn't try to stop them; they could have shot you."

"Well, I didn't exactly sit and do nothing like I was told."

"What do you mean?" BeeBee asked.

I leaned forward. "Did you do something dangerous?"

"I stayed out of sight, don't worry." He crossed his arms, braced for an argument. "I couldn't very well let them shoot up your apartment and leave though. I may have put my car in neutral and pushed it in the general direction of the rear of theirs." Landon's lips twitched.

"You blocked them in?"

"Don't worry. I wasn't in my car, I made sure it would roll up behind them and then I hid behind another vehicle until the cops came. The idiots could have gotten out of their car and run, but instead, they just kept trying to back up." His brows creased. "Though I probably should have told dispatch my plan because for a minute, I thought that cop was going to shoot me when I stepped out of hiding."

"I thought so, too." A deep voice rumbled from the doorway.

My head whipped around and then up. And up. How did a giant of a man like that appear without so much as a peep? Considering the fact that he had to duck half an inch to come through my doorway, I estimated the police officer to be pushing seven and a half feet tall. He must have been the partner, now finished working the scene downstairs.

"Thank for not shooting our friend," BeeBee said when the quiet had moved to the awkward stage.

"Which of you is Miss Rivers?" The officer didn't acknowledge the comment. His face sported a mask of professionalism; still, I couldn't help but think he appeared uncomfortable crammed in my tiny kitchen.

"I am."

"I need you to come with me, ma'am."

BeeBee's eyes widened in fear. I forget, with her previously lifestyle there's no telling what her experience with cops has been like. I smiled and squeezed her hand, offering reassurance that I'll be fine.

Landon began to stand, but the officer waved him back. "This will only take a moment. After we're done, I'll escort Miss Rivers right back here." He glanced at BeeBee then back at Landon. I took it to mean he wanted Landon to stay and make sure BeeBee stayed put because Landon gave a brief nod and settled back into his chair.

I followed the officer through the broken door of my apartment into the parking lot, trying not to gawk. A hard thing to do when my head barely reached above his elbow. What in the world did his mama feed this man as a child?

Red and blue lights still swirled, but the sirens were no longer blaring. Two long white sheets lay across the ground. I didn't have a good feeling about this. "Sir, what is it you needed from me exactly?"

"Sheriff Kent radioed over after hearing dispatch send us to your place over the radio. He suggested you might be able to identify one of the shooters." He pointed his long arm toward the ghostly sheets several feet away.

Identify the perp. The body, he means. I clenched my hands by my side and close my eyes. Counting. Praying. Steeling myself. "Do I...do I have to touch it?" I pointed at the sheet.

The officer loosened his stance. "No, ma'am. You tell me when you're ready," his rumbling voice softened. "I'll pull the sheet down just enough for you to look at the face and torso and put it right back. Quick as can be, then we'll get you back to your friends."

I jerked my head in a quick nod and walked forward. Even with a few steps head start, the officer passed me and was waiting, giant hands poised on the corner of the cloth. "Okay," I said.

With a flick of the wrists, he folded the sheet neatly below the shoulders of the man on the ground. I searched the face. Tried humming in my head to tune out the blood. Glanced at the arms and turned away, shaking my head. "I don't know him. Haven't seen him before." The man had no tattoos on his neck and only a large tiger visible on one of his sleeveless shoulders.

The gentle giant next to me moved on, hands at the ready on the second sheet. "Best to get it over with," he told me. "Ready?"

I rub my hands across my face, blow out a breath and agree. "Let's do it." The sheet whipped back and I hugged my arms across myself. It was him. Susumu, intricate tattoos dancing across his body, lay motionless. His tan face looked paler, empty; his body just a shell. I stepped away.

"Well?"

"That is the man who has been trying to kill me. His name is Susumu Takumi. At least," I added wryly, "to the best of my knowledge. He didn't seem interested in introductions the first time that I saw him."

"Thank you, Miss Rivers. That is all we need."

~

Ages later, or a scant forty-five minutes if the clock on the stove was to be believed, I hauled the strap of my duffle bag over my shoulder and looked around my home. The anger had come and gone, maybe not completely gone, but with Susumu dead, there wasn't anyone for me to take it out on anyway. The shock would probably surface later.

For now, well, for now, it seemed unbelievable that anyone could purposefully inflict this kind of damage. I sifted through my emotions, pushing aside the worry about what the cleanup would entail, banishing the little part of me that wanted to throw a party because Susumu had been killed by the police, and chose to embrace gratitude that once again God had protected me, protected BeeBee, and had given me good friends to help me through this insanity.

I joined BeeBee and Landon on the front stoop. "I'm ready to go."

"What about the door?" BeeBee asked.

I pointed to the cruiser pulling into the parking lot. "Sheriff Kent reassigned the deputy watching Besuto Auto Repair to sit here for the night and make sure nobody breaks in. I think he brought some boards or something to temporarily seal the place up. The rest, I'll deal with tomorrow." Fighting exhaustion as the adrenaline drained from my system, I trudged toward my truck. The plan was to drop Landon off at a hotel near Sam and Griff's place since his car was out of commission.

"You have court tomorrow."

I sighed at the reminder. "Then I'll deal with it on Tuesday. Right now, I don't want to look at any of it any longer."

Chapter 28

"Why did you wait until morning to tell me all of this?" Sam's outraged expression made me cringe.

"I know, I know. Best friends are supposed to wake up infinitely concussed best friends and render them sleepless by explaining all the scary details of another near-death experience so that nobody in the house gets any rest." I let the sarcasm linger in the air, pursing my lips. It really wasn't right to have to start Monday off by getting scolded.

"Yes. Exactly." Sam crossed her arms. "Where do you think the saying 'misery loves company' came from anyway? Probably some set of friends who constantly kept the other worried and tired by telling each other all of their problems. Just like friends are *supposed* to do."

"I'm not going to argue with you."

"Because you know I'm right."

"Because I have to get dressed for court."

"I already picked out some clothes for you," Sam said like I shouldn't be worrying over something so silly. "They're over there on the couch."

My phone beeped. I looked down at it and then narrowed my eyes at Sam. "Did you tell Gladys?"

"BeeBee, do you want some more coffee?" Sam focused everywhere but on me at that moment.

"Do you know what you've done?" I asked. "Gladys is texting me a whole new list of things she thinks we need as supplies."

Sam concentrated on stirring cream into BeeBee's coffee cup, half a teaspoon at a time.

Exasperated, I threw my hands in the air and walked over to the couch, grabbing my clothes. "I'm leaving," I said less than ten minutes later. My hair was in its usual messy bun and I opted out of makeup. If I were going to testify, I would be comfortable in my own skin doing it. Thankfully, Sam had been considerate of the day ahead of me and picked out professional but oh-so-comfy slacks and a loose peasant top blouse. If there were a breeze in the courtroom, I would feel it. Besides, I'd been almost buried alive, shot at, and exposed to more dead bodies than I ever cared to see again. Let me talk in front of some people – piece of cake. *Mmm cake.*

"Cake."

"What?" Sam raised an eyebrow at me. Even BeeBee tilted her head in confusion.

"When court is over, or I'm dismissed, whatever the process is, I want cake. A really, really big chocolate cake with peanut butter frosting." I licked my lips and grinned.

"You're so weird," Sam winked.

"OMG!" BeeBee exclaimed.

I chuckled, seeing that Victoria and Millie were rubbing off on her already.

"What?"

"We forgot to tell Sam about the really good news!"

Sam groaned. "More news?" She clasped her head in her hands. "I'm not sure I can take any more news from you two."

"You'll like this," I promised. "Go ahead, tell her." I nodded at BeeBee.

"Flo sold over 150 orders thanks to the Fourth of July promotional. Millie says that means you have to do your hair patriotic!" BeeBee did a little dance in her chair. "So. What are you going to do?"

"I'm going to call my stylist that's what." Sam grinned and grabbed her phone, heading to her room. "Crank the truck," she called over her shoulder. "I'll be right there."

We met Landon at his hotel before we left Seashell Bay; he had offered to escort BeeBee for a taxi ride to get her to work at Flo's on time.

~

"All rise." I stood along with the others present in the courtroom as the judge entered.

Sam had refused to give us any details on her upcoming hair makeover on the ride to court. If possible, it looked like more people were in the courtroom today than there were last week.

I waved a little paper fan in front of my face, making small motions, trying not to be noticed.

Sam leaned toward me and whispered, "Victoria is making your cake."

I raised my eyebrows, sitting back down as the judge told the room we could be seated.

"But if you pass out, I get to eat the whole thing and you can't have any." She leaned back in her seat with a cocky smirk.

I all but growled at her. Growling in court though, they might lock me up for insanity instead of obstruction. The back door opened and Sheriff Kent entered. I watched him have a word with Officer Campbell, who scowled but nodded at whatever Sheriff Kent had to say.

Catching my gaze, the sheriff gave a slight nod before settling into a seat in the back of the room. I refocused my attention to the front of the court. All witnesses were ordered out of the room, same as last time. I found a place on the bench in the hallway closest to the door. The first person called to testify was Alice, the woman in charge of the cleaning crew at The Cove's Cabins.

When Alice came back, she was being escorted by a uniformed officer and they stepped into a smaller room down the hall. I didn't have time to wonder about Alice's fate; they called my name next.

Slow breaths, in and out. I coached myself all the way down the aisle and into the witness box. I took a seat, pleased to see that my hands were still. No shaking.

"Please stand and state your name for the record." Judge Rickson looked down at me.

"My name is Piper Rivers."

"Do you swear to tell the truth, the whole truth, and nothing but the truth?"

"I so swear."

"You may be seated."

I sat again. So far, so good. *Just remember Piper: cake.* Okay, I'm not really that terrible of a person. I came to testify for justice, not for cake. Cake just happened to be a tangible bonus awaiting me.

The prosecutor came forward, I think his name was Thomas but I couldn't recall if that was a first or last name, and addressed the jury. I listened with one ear, not really concerned with them but with my own breathing. I didn't feel dizzy; a good sign if ever there was one. The speech to the jury included a list of all the things the prosecution intended to prove against Regina Wilson today. Murder, abduction, and trafficking in people appeared to be the biggest ones. But who's counting?

"Miss Rivers,' Thomas rounded on me. "I understand you were abducted and held captive against your will by Regina Wilson?"

"Yes, sir."

"When did this occur?"

"Last weekend, the 23rd of June, when I was trying to find my friends Landon and Griff."

"And did you find these two friends?" Thomas pressed.

"I did. Regina had them tied up in a room at the Thai Massage Parlor in Lion's Cove." Focus on Thomas. He's just one person. Ignore the others in the room. I can do this. I am doing this. Elation bubbled up in me as I realized my nervousness had vanished. I didn't feel ill or worried. I intended to tell my whole story and find peace from this nightmare. Regina would get whatever the court determined.

Thomas spoke again and I listened more closely. "I believe you presented evidence to Officer Campbell with a confession by Regina Wilson?"

"Yes, sir. A voicemail on my phone. I emailed the file to Officer Campbell, but it went missing."

"Do you still have the voicemail."

"I do."

"Is it present in this court."

"It is."

"Your honor," Thomas tilted his face up to the judge. "I move that the cell phone of Piper Rivers and voicemail within be accepted as evidence, exhibit A."

"Motion accepted." Judge Rickson tapped his gavel on a round wooden plate.

Thomas held out his hand and I turned over my cell phone into his waiting palm.

"Your honor, I would like to play this voicemail evidence for the jury to hear."

"You may." Judge Rickson inclined his head.

Thomas stepped over to the witness box and twisted the long microphone to the side, away from me. Handing the phone back, he asked that I access my voicemail for him.

"Ladies and gentlemen of the jury," he addressed the room while I fiddled with the buttons entering my code. "What you are about to hear is an admission of guilt from Regina Wilson herself. Please listen carefully." Thomas took the phone back from me and pressed play, holding the speaker close to the microphone.

Old message the phone chirped. Then the voicemail played, loudly and condemningly:

"Hello," Regina's voice spoke. *"I just knew you would call. Listen carefully."*

"Who is this?" my voice snapped.

A muffled sound.

"Regina, where is Griff? And Alice?"

"I'll ask the questions here," Regina barked over the phone. "What did Alice tell you?"

"Nothing. We never got to speak with her. Did you set the cabin fire?"

"Aren't you a smart little cookie; if you keep your mouth shut, then nobody has to get hurt."

My voice again, angry. "Nobody else, you mean? Last time that I checked, two people are dead."

"And isn't that unfortunate. Unless you want it to be your boyfriends here, you'll do as I say."

"What do you want, Regina?" my voice held a small tremble.

"I want you to go bake your crummy desserts tonight and act normal. Don't go poking your nose where it doesn't belong. Tomorrow, I'll send instructions where you can find your friends and that idiot cleaning woman with the big mouth." The voicemail ended. Regina had hung up on me that day.

Silence hung thick in the air. Thomas took his time closing the phone and placing it before the judge, letting the conversation sink in for everyone present. If there had been crickets chirping, we would have heard them loud and clear.

The defense asked for a recess. I was led to wait in a separate area with the other witnesses. My stomach growled. Glancing at my watch, I saw that it was getting close to eleven. Maybe I should have grabbed more than a donut for breakfast.

Half an hour passed before the bailiff returned to collect us. We filed into the courtroom and took seats on the benches. I squeezed back into the row with Sam. Griff had arrived late at some point; I noticed him sitting by Sheriff Kent in the back.

"All rise."

We stood as Judge Rickson entered from his chambers. I looked around. All of the witnesses were present. That must mean there would be no more testimony today. I wondered if the defense had demanded another recess.

"Court is in session." Judge Rickson tapped his gavel once. "You may be seated."

"Your honor, permission to approach the bench."

"Counsel may approach," the judge agreed, nodding to the defense attorney.

I found myself leaning forward, as if I might catch snippets of the private conversation, and forced myself to sit back. Being able to hear anything from here was impossible, anyway. After a few moments, the judge nodded and the defense attorney returned to sit beside Regina.

"Regina Wilson, it is the court's understanding that you wish to enter a plea of guilty. Is this correct?"

"Yes, your honor."

"Do you understand that by entering a plea of guilty, you waive your rights to file any further motions and your right to appeal?"

"I do, your honor."

"Does the prosecution understand and agree with the nature of this plea agreement?" The judge looked at Thomas.

Thomas stood. "The prosecution agrees, your honor." With a nod to the judge and the defense attorney, he sat back down, folding his hands in his lap.

I looked at Sam, a silent question. She shrugged, not sure what was going on either.

Judge Rickson picked up his gavel. "Let the record show that on this date, Regina Wilson enters a plea of guilty to one count of first-degree murder, one count of second-degree murder, five counts of kidnapping, and conspiracy to traffic in persons. Regina Wilson, per the plea agreement made today, you are hereby sentenced to three consecutive life sentences, without the chance of parole." The gavel banged and Judge Rickson swept regally off the stand, robe flowing, and returned to his chambers.

A buzz of conversation erupted all around. I sat, stunned. It was over.

Making our way out of the crowded courtroom took a while. When at last we reached the lobby, Sam, and I were able to catch up to Griff and Sheriff Kent.

Griff wrapped me in a giant hug, planting a kiss on my cheek. "You did great," he squeezed me tighter.

"You really did," Sam agreed.

"Thanks. Does that mean I get cake?"

BeeBee doubled over laughing as Sam rolled her eyes. "Yes, you get a cake."

"Good. I'm starving." I smiled, then grew serious. "What happened though? I thought several more witnesses had to testify and the jury would come to a verdict. Why did Regina plea?"

"You really don't know?" Sheriff Kent cocked his head.

"Know what?"

"That voicemail you saved had Regina dead to rights admitting to two murders. Add that to the list of other charges and she was easily facing the death penalty, which her defense attorney was smart enough to recognize when he heard the recording." Sheriff Kent rocked on his heels. "They cut a deal with the prosecution right after to have the death penalty taken off the table if she confessed. I don't know for a fact, but if I were the prosecutor, I would have also insisted on names or other evidence for the trafficking charges."

Understanding, I nodded. "So. Regina will live the rest of her life in federal prison, but she'll live." The sheriff nodded. "What about Susumu and talking to Campbell about her being helpful?"

"I told him about that case, but technically none of Regina's information resulted in the apprehension of the criminal. He wasn't found at either of the location's that she gave up."

"Makes sense. One other thing confused me. Why didn't Alice ever come back after she gave testimony?"

Able to answer that one, Sam spoke first. "Alice admitted to knowingly engaging in labor trafficking. Regina supplied her with women for the

291

cleaning crew and Alice barely paid them. Regina threatened to put them back into massage parlors if Alice was ever unhappy with their service."

"How awful!" I would never understand treating people as if they were a commodity instead of a human being.

"I've got to get back to my own county now," the sheriff shook Griff's hand and waved bye to the rest of us.

Griff took his leave as well. "I've got a few buildings to see to today," he told us. "I'll check in later."

"How are you feeling, Piper?" Sam asked me quietly as we walked across the parking lot to my truck.

I considered the question. I knew Sam was asking physically; she was glad I hadn't passed out but still concerned. The truth was, I felt fine. About all of it. "I feel good," I said honestly. "I did a good thing today, and a woman who hurt countless people will never be free to do so again. I faced a fear of mine and overcame it. We don't have to worry about Susumu popping out of the woodwork to attack anymore. It's like the sun came out after a rainy afternoon."

"Plus, there is about to be cake."

I grinned and hugged Sam to my side. "Plus, there's that."

We got into the truck and I cranked it up. I started to turn up the volume, but Sam reached out and stopped me.

"I forgot. There is one piece of bad news."

My mind spun over the possibilities as I waited for Sam to speak. When she didn't, I sat back and turned to face her in my seat. "Well?"

"You may die – when you see my patriotic hair this weekend!"

I covered my head in my hands as Sam cracked up laughing. "Cruel. You're just a cruel woman," I told her. "I thought something terrible had happened at the bakery or that your Post-Concussion Syndrome might be getting worse." I shook my head. "When is your hair appointment?"

"Thursday. Oh, that reminds me - yours is tomorrow. To get your ends touched up." Sam smiled.

Chapter 29

From the courthouse, I drove us straight to the bakery. Victoria was alone in the kitchen when Sam unlocked the back door for us to go inside.

"Hey!" Sam greeted in a sing-song voice.

She sounded so cheerful and normal that I almost clapped. I'd been watching her closely for the twinging and creased brows that had been present even when she was trying to hide the headaches; so far today, I hadn't seen any signs of them. I hoped with all my heart that meant she wouldn't have to suffer any further effects from the concussion.

"Y'all are earlier than I thought you would be," Victoria smiled. "I'm glad you're both back though. We've missed you." She loaded the last dish into the dishwasher then turned to hug us. "How are you doing, Sam?"

"I'm wonderful, thank you for asking."

"And Piper? How did court go?"

"Do you have time for a break?" I asked her. She gave a quick nod. "Then let's go up front so that I can tell you and Gladys at the same time," I suggested.

~

"Good riddance," Gladys summed up her opinion with one phrase. She had listened as Sam and I recounted the morning's events. "You best go tell Flo and the others now," she told me.

"Don't you want me to stay and help?" I asked. "I haven't even checked with Victoria to see what baking we need to catch up on."

"I've got it covered," Victoria assured me as she pushed back through the swinging door and disappeared into the kitchen.

"I'll do some cleaning while Sam takes a turn at the counter," Gladys insisted.

"I can clean," Sam frowned.

"No. Those chemicals may give you a headache and you've had enough of those." Gladys refused to even consider it.

Halfway to the front door, I paused. A new addition was perched by the door. "Gladys. What is this?" I pointed to the short, potted palm.

"Mina."

"Pardon me?"

"That's Mina," she said. "She's a mini-palm. I thought you could use someone to stand guard."

I looked back at the little palm, stooping to see below the large leaves. I gave a startled laugh; a little face stared back at me, one eyebrow arched and looking uncannily like Sam. "Thank you, Gladys." I couldn't wait to show Mina to Griff. And BeeBee! I forgot that she didn't know about Gladys's carving talent yet. I stepped out onto the sidewalk and inhaled the salty air as I made the short walk to Flo's Flowers.

When I stepped inside the shop, the scent on the air changed; gone was the sharp and salty, replaced by a soft and floral smell. BeeBee worked behind the counter, jotting down things on an order form for an older gentleman. I stepped aside to let him pass when he finished.

He nodded his thanks. "You kids have a nice day," he said as he plodded toward the door.

I grinned. It'd been a long time since anyone referred to me as a kid.

"I'll get Flo and Millie," BeeBee said instantly. "We've all been waiting to hear from you."

I strolled around the room, admiring the beautiful flowers and taking the time to look for varieties I hadn't seen before until I heard the three come in from the back. After I told them how things had gone at court, I asked about the business. "Have new sales continued to be good?"

"Incredible," Flo smiled at the turn things had taken in such a short time. "I think most of the town has been in here," she marveled.

"Seashell Bay takes holidays pretty seriously," I observed. "Maybe we can think of other big promos throughout the year to keep things steady."

"At this rate, I'll be able to hire full-time help around here soon," Flo sat down on a stool behind the counter and tugged off one of her shoes. "I may have to buy some thicker floor mats though. All this standing to arrange so many more flowers than usual has done a number on my feet."

"Let me see them," BeeBee reached for the closest sock-covered foot and began pressing and kneading before Flo could protest.

"No, you don't have to...oh!" Flo closed her eyes. "You're good at this. How did you know where it hurts?"

BeeBee shrugged. "I just thought it might help. Here, I'll rub the other one."

I wondered at the kindness that had survived in this girl when I doubted very little kindness had been shown to her. "You know," I mused out loud. "BeeBee is hoping to get a job at the spa at the end of the year. I bet she could use the practice between now and then. She can't technically charge for foot rubs or back rubs, but she can't stop us from giving her tips either."

"Write me down for a weekly foot massage," Flo said without hesitation as she pulled her shoes back on and stood. "For now, it's back to work we go."

Before she could leave, the door opened and in stepped Gladys, Sam and Victoria. Victoria carried a platter with several generous slices of cake on it. "What are you all doing here?" I asked.

Griff and Landon squeezed into the room behind them. "Are we late?" Griff asked.

"Ta-da!" Victoria and Sam exclaimed.

I looked more closely at the cake. Chocolate cake. "Is that...?"

"Peanut butter frosting," Victoria answered with a nod. "And inside are chopped bits of peanut butter cups."

"Who's watching the bakery?" I hated to seem ungrateful, but worry niggled at my brain.

"Don't worry," Gladys waved her hand. "We left the rest of the cake sliced into tiny squares as free samples in the middle of the room. Nobody's passing that up," she winked. "The whole group will still be happy as a hog in mud when we're done here."

"And we will go back over there as soon as we share a slice with you," Sam promised. Probably to prevent a mini-heart attack on my part.

"I lucked out with the best friends in the world!" I accepted my slice of cake and plastic fork.

"You haven't heard the best part," Victoria looked over at Griff and Landon.

Everyone seemed to be smiling at some secret that I didn't know. "If it's better than cake, somebody better tell me because I can't fathom it getting better than this." I licked frosting off of my fork and looked around expectantly.

"Goodness, I'll tell her. These two," Gladys did her best Vanna White impersonation from Wheel of Fortune by waving her arms around Griff and Landon, "repaired your apartment from the door down to the sweeping."

My jaw dropped and my plate nearly followed.

Griff nodded, shuffling on his feet. "It's just waiting for you to pick out some new paint colors."

"Sam suggested the two of you could go shopping. Maybe redecorate a little while you're at it," Landon glanced at Sam, his gaze lingering, then looked back at me. "Everything else is good to go like Griff said."

"I don't know what to say," tears welled in my eyes. "Thank you so much! I don't know how you even had time to do that, but thank you."

Chapter 30

Back into our busy routines, the week flew by smoothly and Friday snuck up on us before we knew it. Our largest disaster occurred on Wednesday when we ran out of dark chocolate chips for the first time in history. Gladys and Sam implied that the double handfuls I'd been throwing back every hour or so had something to do with that but I ignored the insinuations.

Here we were baking up a storm, boxing up to-go orders, and readying to close early so that we could each go to the Independence Day Parade. The Fourth had finally arrived and excitement buzzed in the air.

"Have you seen Sam yet?" It was the third time that I'd been asked that question this morning. First by Victoria, then Millie, now Gladys. It seemed most of today's anticipation hinged on seeing Sam's new hair color than on the Independence Day Parade later today.

"No."

"And you have no idea what she meant by patriotic hair?"

"Not a clue. It must be pretty wild though."

"Hmmm. Maybe she bought a wig." Gladys looked thoughtful.

"I don't think so," I shook my head. "She made an appointment at the salon. Not to mention, I've seen Sam sport some pretty crazy colors and still, she said I would die when I saw her hair today."

Gladys beat out a drum roll on the kitchen island where we sat awaiting Sam to make her grand entrance. "I can't wait. I should have colored my hair, too."

The clock showed seven; much later than her normal arrival to the bakery and I hoped nothing was wrong. She told me she would be late, but not how late.

A key scraped in the lock and I rushed to the back door, unlocking it from the inside and flinging it open.

"Oh. My. Gosh." Victoria's phrase leaped to my mouth, the only thing I could think to say.

"Let me see, let me see."

I stepped aside, giving Sam room to enter so that Gladys could see. Victoria appeared from the walk-in fridge. They both froze in place.

"What do you think?" Sam spun as if we couldn't already see the outrageous new hair. Her long locks were not one, not two, but three colors. Yep. She did it. Red, white, and blue hair.

"It's definitely patriotic," I told her as I studied her. Parted in the middle, one half of her hair was a deep red. The other half was white from the root down to about four inches from the bottom where a royal blue color took over to the ends.

"Wow! My mother would kill me if I did that to my hair," Victoria's eyes widened to nearly the size of dessert plates.

"I approve." Gladys clapped her hands.

"Your mother may not kill you," I told Sam. "But don't you think this might be the last straw that makes her keel over and die of embarrassment and disappointment?"

Sam laughed. "It may do just that. So. Are you going to come with me and film her reaction when I greet her and Dad on the courthouse lawn before the Independence Day parade tonight?"

I gave my best evil cackle followed by a wide grin. "You better believe it!"

Note from the Author

Hey there! Thank you again, wonderful readers, for coming back for book 3. Piper and Sam would be so sad without you.

Keep reading for a sneak peek at book 4!

Also, did you know you can sign up for my newsletter to receive updates and deals before anyone else? **My newsletter subscribers even took a survey and helped me choose the title of book #4.** Does that sound like something you want to get in on? If so, go to the following link in your web browser and sign up for my newsletter now!

If you have enjoyed the books, I would really appreciate you leaving a review on Amazon, Goodreads, or BookBub as well. Reviews are a great way to help my book reach other readers like yourself.

Thanks again!

Sincerely,

Katherine

Book 4 Sneak Peek: Savory, Sweet, & Scandalous

"Where's Gladys?" I asked Sam as I entered the Ooey Gooey Goodness bakery café through the swinging kitchen door.

"Two guesses."

I thought about it a moment; today was Friday. "I don't know. Cooking class?" I lifted my arms, palms face up, in a *who knows* gesture.

Sam gave me a thumbs up. "Ding, ding, ding. We have a winner."

"I don't know what to think about the fact that she never brings Chef Fabio here."

"Frédéric," Sam corrected me automatically. Fabio, we had learned from Gladys, was part of his cooking persona title but not his actual name.

"Right. Hey, weren't cooking classes supposed to be over last week?"

"What are you saying?"

I waggled my eyebrows at Sam suggestively. "I'm saying, I think we've moved from assisting in cooking classes to actual date nights and someone is embarrassed to tell us."

"Maybe so." Sam chewed on her bottom lip, a habit I was shocked had survived her childhood with Sam's mother, Deidra, pushing her in and out of etiquette classes, ladylike behaviors, and so on. "Well? Are we going to snoop?" Sam rubbed the palms of her hands together.

"We can't snoop with your hair like that; it's a beacon to everyone around. If Gladys didn't spot us herself, everyone else talking about the woman with red, white, and blue hair would tip her off that we were following her." I shook my head. Sam had outdone herself with her promise to dye her hair *patriotic* as an incentive to boost sales at Flo's Flowers and the Ooey Gooey Goodness Bakery a few weeks ago, right before the Independence Day Parade.

"Are you saying you think it's time to change it?" she fingered the white and blue strands on one side of her head.

"I'm only pointing out that it isn't exactly clandestine snooping material."

"Good point. I guess it might be time to change it. It has been worth it to see the pained expression on Mother's face whenever I'm around though."

I laughed. Deidra Lowe had nearly fainted on the spot when Sam appeared on the courthouse lawn beside them on July Fourth. Deidra's pallor had first gone ashy-white and then flushed a deep crimson. Sam's father hadn't even had time to say hello before Deidra shooed us out of the spotlight. So determined was she to send Sam away before the press arrived, that she nearly broke an ankle in a gopher hole rushing us away from the courthouse steps. I pity the poor gophers who called that lawn their home; Deidra had been on a crusade to capture and kill every gopher in a five-mile radius ever since.

"Earth to Piper!" Sam spoke, breaking through my thoughts.

"Hmm?"

"Are you going to come with me to the salon? You could get your hair touched up."

I considered it, holding the ends of my hair up right in front of my nose. Tipped in turquoise and silver, the ends of my hair were definitely sporting some major split ends. She was right; it was time to trim and re-color the ends. Before I could answer, the bell over the door jingled, signaling a customer entering.

The Ooey Gooey Goodness Bakery, owned and operated by myself and Sam, had become more and more popular over the last few weeks, thanks in part to a publicized fundraising campaign to raise awareness of human trafficking, and then, more recently, to a promotional strategy where we joined forces with Flo's Flowers next door to increase Fourth of July flower and cookie orders. Still, the last hour had been dead; we had been about to close up. I looked over, quite surprised, to see who might be coming in for a cookie this late.

My jaw dropped. Speak of the devil.

"Mother?" Sam asked, eyebrows raised in disbelief.

As long as we had owned the Ooey Gooey, Deidra had not set foot inside. Until today. One time, only one, she had sent an assistant over to place a cookie order but it had been more about PR for her than support of us. This didn't bode well.

"Good evening, Mrs. Lowe," the greeting felt thick and awkward even as it slid over my tongue. "Can we get you something?"

Deidra glowered. Her fist clenched tighter around a folded newspaper in her hand. "How dare you?"

I swiveled my head to Sam. She looked at me in confusion then back to her mother.

"How dare who, what?" Sam blew out a breath. Deidra's penchant for drama wasn't new in her life.

"This, this…." Deidra stalked forward. She waved her free hand in a circle, motioning to Sam's head, or rather her hair. "This atrocity is more than enough to bring embarrassment to your father and I. But you couldn't stop there, could you?"

"Mrs. Lowe," I stepped up beside Sam, wrapping an arm around her shoulders. "I don't think anyone is judging you for Sam's hair color. Really."

"You. You stay out of this. You've done enough to drag my children down into some mediocre, ambitionless life. This doesn't concern you." Her eyes flashed daggers at me. I felt Sam stiffen at my side.

"Get out."

"Excuse me?" Deidra's voice grew cold.

I whipped my head to face Sam, concerned as I felt her begin to shake.

"Get out and don't come back. I don't know what it is you think I've done, but you will not come in our bakery and be disrespectful to me or my best friend. Don't let the door hit you on the way out." Sam crossed her arms, matching her mother stare for stare.

"Well. Don't think we are finished, young lady. This is far from over." Deidra shoved the paper into Sam's folded arms and stormed out, high-heel pumps tapping out the drum beats of impending war on her way.

Coming Soon!

Look for Book 4 in the Ooey Gooey Bakery Mystery series late summer 2019.

Also, Piper and Sam will be starring in a fun little short story full of humor and furniture shopping in *Couches and Catastrophes.*

After that, hang on to your hats because Gladys is getting her own series!

Other Books by Katherine Brown

Ooey Gooey Bakery Mystery Series:

Rest, Relax, Run for Your Life

Pastries, Pies, & Poison

School is Scary Series (Children)

Kindergarten Teachers are Witches

Fingernails of First Grade

Second Grade Stinks

Third Grade's Terrible Trip

Fourth Grade's Fossil Find

Fairy Tale Retellings

Marigold and the Bear Necessities

Cloaked

Other Children's Books

Princess Bethani's First Garden Party

www.ingramcontent.com/pod-product-compliance
Lightning Source LLC
Chambersburg PA
CBHW071203100726
47908CB00002B/491